I0668050

BLACK & WHITE CROAKIES

SAM CHEEVER

ELECTRIC PROSE PUBLICATIONS

Good parenting advice: Only allow your small frog, cat, and hobgoblin limited and supervised television time, or risk stunting their mental and physical growth.

Yeah, it might already be too late for that...

It seemed like good, innocent fun. A trip back to a simpler time, a fun jaunt to the "good old days". It turned out to be anything *but* harmless. The "kids" loved the old, black and white shows. But, per usual at Croakies, things devolved quickly, transforming "quiet" time into a heart-pounding adventure.

And of course, as you'd expect, the frog, the cat, and the hobgoblin are right in the middle of it all.

I'm a total derf at this whole parenting thing.

And my "children" are brats.

Holy flippin' frog flatulence. So much for the good old days...

1

WE NEED TO TALK

"They're staring at that old TV again," Sebille informed me as she came into the bookstore from the artifact library.

I shrugged, tucking a curly strand of long brown hair behind my ear. I was secretly happy the terrible threesome wasn't flinging flour around the bookstore or creating more of those bunny-butted songbirds that had all but overrun Croakies. I'd had to hide the Plex hand vac from Hobs, my resident hobgoblin, because every time he used it to suck up dirt, the thing made more songbirds. They were currently lined two deep along the tops of my bookshelves, pooping all over the pretty new wood shelves beneath their feathered boohinds.

I had so many of the annoyingly happy critters in the store that I'd had to create a birdseed column in my monthly expenses.

"It's not hurting them," I said, the goddess of rationalization. "And it keeps them out of trouble."

Sebille glared over at me, her bright green gaze narrowed. "They need to turn it off and go use their imaginations or something," said the cranky sprite, whose parenting instincts had heretofore been inspired mostly by the pithy little sayings in the fortune cookies she so loved.

The tiny amalgamate dragon perched on Sebille's shoulder chittered happily, lifting her wings and flying across the room to visit with her friends the songbirds. The birds broke into happy song at the dragon's arrival. Little Sadie lifted her tiny head and joined them. Sebille and I winced. The dragon's "song" sounded more like screeching banshees than music.

Luckily, there were so many birds they mostly overwhelmed the dragon's voice.

Silver lining.

A whistling theme song rose above the bird's clatter, as if Hobs was trying to drown out the happy noise by turning up the volume on the elderly TV. I recognized the song from a very old sitcom, which involved a country sheriff and his bumbling deputy dealing with a lot of silly problems.

Since I'd recently been lost in a dimensional wrinkle; had almost been killed by monsters, wizards, and demons more than once; and have had to continually deal with a naughty hobgoblin, a magical cat, and a snarky talking frog; I'd give almost anything to have problems as mundane as who was going to tell Aunt Bee her new rhubarb pie tasted like butt.

I'm just sayin'.

The door to my recently updated store opened, and a small elderly woman came inside, her eyes going wide as she took in the renovations. "Oh my! It looks lovely, dear."

I embraced Mrs. Foxladle, my favorite human customer. At just a little over five feet tall, she seemed diminutive next to my five feet nine inches. "Thank you, Mrs. F! It's so nice to see you. It's been a while."

Behind me, the dividing door closed softly. "Hello, Mrs. F," Sebille said, waving as she headed toward the tea counter. "Can I make you some tea?"

"No, thank you, Sebille dear. I won't be but a minute." She squeezed my hand. "I've been a bit under the weather."

"Oh, no. Nothing serious, I hope?"

"Just a cold, dear. No worries. And then the store was closed for a couple of weeks." She looked around. "I barely recognize the place." Despite her kind words, her expression was dubious.

"I know it's shocking. But this old place was long overdue for a facelift." *Especially after being trashed by an epic battle against monsters from the abyss*, I thought. But, of course, I wouldn't tell Mrs. F that.

"I kind of liked its old, saggy face." She chuckled, reassuring me that her statement wasn't a criticism so much as a statement of fact. "When you get older like me, you find comfort in timeworn, familiar things. Do you know I've been coming to this wonderful store for twenty years?"

My blue eyes went wide. "Seriously?"

"Seriously." She gave me a mischievous look. "I'm glad you didn't replace that old sign outside. It always makes me smile."

I barely kept from rolling my eyes. I'd tried several times to update that stupid sign when I'd taken over Croakies. The scratched and tattered wooden sign with its ugly spotted frog was apparently under a magical grandfathering clause. Every time I'd tried to put a new sign in its place, or even change the name of the store, the sign had magically reappeared, and the paperwork had mysteriously reverted back to the old name.

I'd given up after several tries, finally deciding that I would try to like the quirky original placard since it seemed I had no choice. "What can I help you with today?" I asked Mrs. Foxladle.

Her gaze skimmed away from mine as if she wasn't sure how her response would be received. "My visit isn't about books, dear. I know you occasionally take in...antiques."

Mrs. Foxladle had seen me handling artifacts a time or two. I hadn't realized she'd noticed them or made a connection about my having them in my possession. The woman might be well into her seventies, but she was still sharp as a tack.

I shrugged, giving her a response that I hoped was suitably vague. "Occasionally, I help friends move things around."

"A friend of mine has been searching for a specific television set. An old black and white one. He collects antique entertainment media. I believe he has an old record player and a VHS player too." She shook her head. "Anyway, my friend Gladys walked by Croakies a couple of days ago and mentioned she'd seen you carrying one inside. I wondered if it was for sale?"

Black and white bat boogers! I suddenly felt like a bug under glass. Apparently, the whole city of Enchanted had been watching my every move.

I shook my head. "I'm sorry. That television belongs to a friend of mine. I'm just storing it for her until she moves into her new place." I really hated to lie to my favorite human, but I couldn't very well tell her the television was a magical artifact. The man we'd taken it from had been human and had apparently gotten it from my favorite giant.

Theopolis Gargantu owned *Enchanted Collateral*, Enchanted's only pawn shop, and he'd evidently had the TV for a few months, lost in the mess of his over-stuffed home artifact.

What is a home artifact, you ask? It's pretty much as it sounds. A giant's residence is a living, breathing entity. A magical artifact. As such, it has a life of its own and you never know what to expect when you walk into one. A giant's home artifact is generally benign. However, like the giants who live in them, the artifacts crave clutter and the accumulation of stuff. And that clutter always seemed to be moving around.

It would be easy for Theo to lose stuff in the clutter. In fact, he often did. The only miracle was that he ever managed to *find* anything in it.

When Theo's customer had come looking for the old relic, Theo had reluctantly decided to sell it to him. Only because the man had offered Theo several items in exchange for the TV. Apparently, as soon as he'd sold the ancient television, Theo'd had second thoughts, probably because he'd suspected the man was human.

Selling magical artifacts to humans was a dangerous practice. Against the laws of the magic governing body, the Société of Dire Magic. And if the Société found out that Theo had sold the artifact, he'd be in a lot of trouble. He might even lose Enchanted Collateral.

Which would all but kill him.

Anyway, when Theo realized the error of his

ways, he'd come to me. He'd given me the man's address and had reluctantly handed me an envelope filled with enough cash to buy it back. Sebille and I had gone to retrieve the television and found the man's door unlocked. The television artifact in the living room had been turned on and showed only black and white snow on its small screen. There'd been no sign of the man. Asking around the neighborhood, we'd gotten assurances that he hadn't been seen for a couple of days. So we'd taken the television from his living room and left the envelope in its place.

On the way back to Croakies, I'd called Detective Wise Grym to request that he check into the man's disappearance. Which reminded me, I needed to check in with my favorite detective.

You know, just to find out if he'd located Mrs. F's missing friend.

What other reason could I possibly have for calling him?

Shush now!

"What's your friend's name?" Sebille asked, carrying over a steaming cup of tea and settling it on the brand-new table in the center of the open area at the front of the shop. Like most everything else, the previous table had been turned into so much kindling during the monster battle.

"Dugan McDonald," Mrs. Foxladle said, smiling shyly. "He's Irish."

Alarm tightened in my chest. I glanced at Sebille and found her widened gaze. That was the name of the man we'd confiscated the television from. "When was the last time you spoke to Mr. McDonald?" I asked Mrs. Foxladle.

She shrugged. "Last Sunday, I think. He goes to my church." She tugged her wool coat close around her throat as if she were cold. I realized when she spoke again that it signified embarrassment. She clearly liked the man a lot and was disconcerted to show it. "He has such a pleasant accent. So lilting. I believe there's romance in accents, don't you, dear?"

"Definitely. Are you sure you wouldn't like to stay for some tea?" I asked, hoping she'd take that as her cue to go. I needed to talk to Sebille about the new information and contact Grym.

"No. But thank you. I need to be going. Are we still on for book club tonight?"

I wanted to say no, but I didn't have the heart to disappoint her. I'd had to cancel her book club meeting for the last several weeks due to my busy schedule and then the renovations. I didn't want to let her down again.

"We're on for seven as planned. I might have to run out for a bit this afternoon, but I should be back in plenty of time."

She inclined her head. "Good. I'm really looking forward to it. Detective Grym has agreed to join us." Her smile was sly. I got the distinct impression the elderly woman had decided it was her job to fix me up with Wise Grym.

I had no intention of being the victim of her matchmaking. There was only so far I'd go to make a customer happy. Even one I liked as much as Mrs. Foxladle. "I'll see you tonight then."

I opened the door for her and found myself staring at the lean, rock-hewn form of a man whose hand was formed as if to grasp the door handle.

It was the devil himself. Or, if you preferred, Detective Grym.

Potato potahto.

Mrs. Foxladle beamed up at him. "There you are young man. We were just talking about you."

Grym took the hand she offered him and smiled down at the tiny woman. "No wonder my ears were ringing," he told her.

She laughed gaily. "We *will* see you tonight, won't we?"

"I wouldn't miss it for the world."

Watching him treat the elderly woman with such gentle kindness burned away another chunk of the anger I was still holding against the detective for outing me to the Société of Dire Magic. My brain knew that he'd only been doing his job when he'd reported some of my missteps as Keeper to the supervising body. But my heart kept telling me that he should have had my back.

Still, he'd stepped in to help me when I'd

recently had a monster problem, and he'd gone to bat for me with the Société when he probably shouldn't have.

He was slowly but surely worming his way back into my good graces.

Grym watched Mrs. Foxladle walk away down the street and then turned to me, the pleasant expression on his handsome face sliding away. "We need to talk."

I pointed to the table where Sebille had been. It was empty but for Sebille's still steaming teacup. "Sit. Do you want tea?"

The sprite was already walking back to the table with two more cups. "I've got it."

Grym took his with a grateful smile and drank half of it in one gulp. I grimaced, wondering if his tongue was made of rock. That tea was hot. "Thanks, Sebille," he said. "What a morning."

I bit back the urge to laugh. "Worse than fighting a bunch of monsters that were escaping through a tear in the abyss?"

He smiled, shaking his head as he sipped his tea. "Not quite, but close." Grym set his cup down on the table and gave me an earnest look. "That television you picked up?"

I sipped, nodding for him to go on.

"You need to put it into the toxic magic vault ASAP."

Slug slobbers! I felt my eyes go wide. "Why?"

The detective scrubbed a big hand over his face, his expression spooked. After everything he'd seen and done as a supernormal cop in a city that was filled with things like witches, dragons, wizards, and giant snake monsters, I wondered what could put that look in his dark-caramel eyes.

He met my gaze. Held it. "What did the living room of that house look like when you picked up the TV?"

Sebille and I shared a look. "Just like any other living room. A bit overcrowded and cluttered."

The sprite nodded. "It smelled like soup."

I wrinkled my nose. It *had* smelled like cabbage soup. Not my favorite smell.

"It wasn't..." Grym looked down at his tea. I wondered at his clear reluctance to tell us what he'd seen. His hesitation was making me really nervous. My gaze slid to the dividing door, and I thought of that theme song that had suddenly blared from the back.

"Everything wasn't black and white?" Grym asked, his face flushing. "Like an old TV show?"

I shook my head. Sebille and I shared a look. "No."

Leeching color from a house was concerning, I thought. But it didn't explain the haunted expression on Grym's handsome face.

"The color leeching was spreading as I stood

there," he went on. "I tried to stay away from it, but it caught the tip of my shoe before I noticed."

He held his foot up so we could see the perfect line that separated the warm brown leather of his shoe from the flat, gray color of the toe.

"Badger boogers!" I exclaimed. "That's not good."

Grym shook his head. "That's not what's got me worried, though. I think that TV did something to McDonald." His haunted gaze lifted to mine. "I think it grabbed him."

That took a beat to soak in. I sat there, blinking at him.

Then horror hit, turning my spine to ice.

I surged from my chair at the same time the sprite did. I ran toward the dividing door and flung it open, surging through before I thought about what might be waiting for us.

The whistling theme song smacked us in the face like a fist. The sound was loud enough to lance my eardrums and make my head pulse. As we came into the room, it sliced off, leaving behind only a heavy silence.

I jolted to a stop, Sebille slamming into my back with a grunt. I swung my gaze around the room, panic flaring to tighten my chest. The center of the giantnormous room was totally devoid of color. Everything within a growing circle of space was black, white, and gray. At the very center of the circle was the retrieved television artifact. But no ancient television show played across its screen. It was just snow. Black, white, and gray spots dancing behind the curved glass face.

Just as it had been when we'd seen it at Dugan McDonald's place.

The floor in front of the television was empty except for the half-eaten remains of a frosted brownie.

Smeared along the edge of the old artifact, as if the person who'd been eating the brownie had tried to hold onto the frame to keep from being pulled inside, were several long streaks of frosting.

Like chocolate claw marks that screamed of fear and desperation.

Grym came up behind me as my knees buckled, my head shaking in denial. "No, no, no, no, no..."

He caught me, holding me upright with a densely muscled arm around my waist. "Naida?"

Tears burned their way down my cheeks. "They're gone," I said, the words emerging thick and rough through my tear-clogged throat.

Without a word, Sebille reached over and clasped my hand in hers. "We'll get them back, Naida."

I just stood there shaking my head. Hobs, Wicked, and Slimy were gone. Probably sucked into that stupid artifact. And it was all my fault.

I was a terrible parent.

"I should have made them go outside to play," I

murmured, feeling as if my world had just crashed and burned beneath my feet. "I should have made them turn it off. I should have..."

I sagged downward. Grym's arm tightened around my middle, and it was the only thing holding me off the floor.

2

MAGICAL OBJECTS TO AVOID AT ALL COSTS

I sat on the stairs leading up to my apartment, staring at the slowly growing colorless area in the center of the artifact library. With Grym's help, Sebille and I had moved as much as we could out of the area, and Lea was working on a specialized witch circle to contain the spread.

Until she could come up with the perfect blend of herbs and magical energy to stop it from spreading completely, she'd thrown down a temporary dampening spell to at least slow it.

I was trying to decide if I should call Madeline Quilleran and beg for her help, when Rustin arrived with little Sadie, the amalgamate dragon, in tow.

I was so depressed it was all I could do to lift my head and nod at him. "Hey," I said, my voice broken from an hour of crying and railing.

Rustin squeezed my shoulder.

Sadie flew over to Sebille and perched on her shoulder, chittering excitedly about something. "Keep her away from the circle, Sebille," I told my assistant unnecessarily.

Sebille offered me an eye roll but didn't tell me I was an idiot. So that was something.

"Tell me what's going on?" the ghost witch said in a soft voice. Like everyone else, his manner was one of walking on eggshells. As if they all thought I'd break apart into a thousand tiny pieces if anybody talked to me.

They could have been right.

I shrugged. "They were just watching the old black and white television over there. Grym stopped by to tell us the man who had it before we took it was missing and that his home had started to lose its colors."

Rustin frowned over at the large, monotone circle across the massive library space. "Like that?"

I nodded, lifting a tearful gaze to Rustin. "Grym thinks the TV took him."

"The man who owned it? How?"

"I don't know." I sniffed, scraping the heel of my hand under my eyes. "Just sucked him inside, I guess. I think..." My voice closed up on me, and I couldn't finish the thought.

"We think Hobs, Wicked, and Slimy have been sucked inside too," Sebille finished for me. She stood a few feet away from us, her bright green gaze locked on the artifact that was causing all the trouble. Sadie was uncharacteristically silent on her shoulder.

I wondered if the little dragon understood the danger in the room, or if she was just reacting to our moods.

"How long did the man have the artifact?" Rustin asked.

"As close as we can figure, only a couple of days. He told Mrs. Foxladle on Sunday that he was looking for one. Theo sold him that," I sent a murderous glare toward the television artifact, "Monday morning."

"And you don't know when he disappeared?"

I shook my head. "We picked this up last night. The kids have been staring at it almost nonstop since then." I felt the urge to smile at the memory of them lined up in front of it, staring in fascination at the really bad black and white shows. "They'd never seen old TV shows before. They were obsessed."

Rustin nodded. "What happened...after?"

I blinked rapidly, trying to understand what he was asking me. "They disappeared," I said almost angrily, feeling as if he was being unusually dense.

He shook his head. "I mean, to the artifact. Did it turn itself off?"

"No," Sebille responded. "It turned the show off, but the screen went to snow." She jerked her chin to show him the snowy screen. None of us had wanted to get close enough to turn it off.

"Then *that* started happening," I said, nodding toward the color-stripped area,

Rustin stared at it a long moment, his expression thoughtful. "I've heard of these kinds of artifacts. I've never seen one in action."

My eyes went wide. "What do you know about them?"

"Not much. Only that the color stripping gets worse the more...er...energy it consumes. And the stripping will continue unless you do something to reduce its energy, like retrieve the vict..." He stopped himself before he said the word "victims" and cleared his throat. "People who've been drawn inside." He frowned. "But the good news is, if you don't turn it off, it won't reset and it can't pull anybody else inside."

The first thing Sebille and I had done when we'd retrieved it at McDonald's house was to turn it off. We'd reset it.

Flying frog flippers.

"That would explain why it started leeching color so quickly here," Sebille muttered. She sent me a haunted look. "It's pulled in lots of new energy over the last couple of days."

Rustin looked as if there was something he wasn't telling me. Something bad.

I shook it off, not really needing any more bad

news. "I'm only interested in how we get them back."

"Do you know?" Sebille asked the ghost witch. Her shimmery green gaze looked dull with worry.

Rustin sighed. "Sorry. I don't really know much about them. But there has to be information in the artifact library, Naida. It *is* an artifact. Have you researched it?"

I hadn't, I was ashamed to admit. I'd been too busy feeling sorry for myself and worrying about my cat, my frog, and my funny little friend.

I pushed wearily to my feet. "I need to do that."

Rustin nodded. "Let me know if I can help. I'll do anything..." He looked into my eyes. "I mean that, Naida. If you need to go in...I'll do whatever I can to help."

"Thanks, Rustin," I told him. "That's really nice of you."

He frowned, shaking his head. "It's not nice," he said, a little angrily.

I blinked in surprise.

"I feel..." He expelled air, scrubbing a hand over his face. "I grew kind of fond of that little green bus. I don't like the idea of losing him."

I wanted to smack myself. Of course he felt bad about Slimy. They'd lived together...really together... for months when Rustin had been cursed into the frog by his evil uncle. "Do you want to help me research this?"

He nodded enthusiastically. "Yes. Please?"

"I need to help too," Sebille said.

Need, not want. I noticed her word choice and commiserated. If I had to sit around thinking about all the terrible things that could be happening to them for much longer...

Doing something had to be better than doing nothing and simply worrying.

I nodded. "Okay, then let's get started."

I shoved the pile of artifact orders aside on Shakespeare's desk and placed my hands, palms down, over the leather blotter in the center. The aged, tooled leather blotter looked like a book. Shakespeare's family sigil was embossed at the center of what would have been the front cover if it were really a book. The family motto was written along the faux spine in faint gold letters. *Non Sanz Droict*.

Not without Right.

Fortunately, as the current Keeper of the Artifacts, I had the right to utilize the magic in the desk to find a book, as had KoAs before me and future Keepers would do after I was gone.

The desk was a great resource. A vast, virtual librarian with an endless inventory. I had only to ask the right question, and the appropriate tome would find its way to me.

The trick was in asking the right question.

The blotter warmed and shifted beneath my palms as I considered the problem. I had no idea what to even call the magic we were dealing with. Color leeching energy? The "television is bad for you" curse? Trans mutational monochrome magic? Color and people eating energy?

"Try time and reality shifting metamorphic energy," Rustin suggested as if reading my mind.

He'd probably just read the blank expression on my face. An art form all its own.

I nodded.

"Desk, give me everything you have on time and reality shifting metamorphic energy objects."

The blotter warmed and shifted beneath my hands, the surface bubbling as if it were working out the problem. Then a flash of light occurred above the blotter, and a chunky volume entitled *Magical Objects to Avoid at all Costs* appeared. The book settled gently onto the scarred leather surface.

Frowning, I glanced at the black leather book, the silvery lettering of its title so faint and the leather so worn the book appeared to be hundreds of years old.

"Well, that title isn't daunting at all," Sebille muttered.

A sense of despair welled up in me, a deepening pool of fear and dread. I suddenly couldn't move from the overwhelming weight of it. "Wicked," I whispered, the word barely squeezing through my clenched throat.

Rustin reached past me and grabbed the book. "Why don't I look at this one."

I nodded, not even bothering to look up.

It took me a moment to realize the blotter was still shifting under my fingers. A beat later, another flash of light produced a second volume on the air before my face. The book looked relatively new, the embossed surface of the red leather cover still shiny and bright. The title on the second tome was *The Case of the Disappearing Artifacts.* Subtitled *Artifacts that Disappear Objects and People.*

"This sounds like exactly what we're looking for," I told the sprite.

Sebille nodded, "Let's see what it says."

I reached out and touched the edge of the heavy leather cover. Before I could open it, the cover flipped open under its own steam and a familiar, if unwelcome, visage rose from the depths of the creamy yellow pages.

The disembodied head turned toward me as it rose, his bright black eyes going slightly wider when he saw us.

It was Doctor Mortimus Osvald, Professor of Devilry at the New York Institute of Magic.

The picture on the first page was of Doctor Osvald's full form, longer and leaner than I would have guessed, though I'd only ever seen his head floating around. In the photo, he was seated casually on a desk, his frame skewed slightly sideways, and a book held in one big hand resting against a long thigh. The man's face was younger in the photo, fractionally less scary, but that was probably only because it was a slightly blurry picture, and it was hard to see the madness in the black eyes.

The head, however, was floating before me in all its glorious madness. The professor's scraggly dark brown hair hung past ears that were pressed tightly against his head and looked almost too small. The hair was stringy as usual, hanging in an untidy fashion against a throat with thick veining, as if someone was pinching him just under the chin to collect the blood there. The skin of his face was its usual ruddy color and looked as if he regularly rubbed it with sandpaper to keep it rough. The full lips pinched into a tight line as he stared back at me, clearly not any happier about our unexpected meeting than I was. "Professor Osvald," I said, narrowing my gaze on him in lieu of a smile. "How are you?"

"Keeper," Osvald said in his arrogant voice, his hostile gaze skimming worriedly over the sprite.

He *might* have reason to look worried.

It was *possible* I might have slammed his book closed a little harder than necessary the last time we'd used one of his many magical reference tomes. And Sebille? Well, let's just say she once threatened to introduce him to a book burning. Up close and personal.

"To what do I owe the dubious pleasure?" Osvald asked in a cool tone.

"No pleasure," I told him, trying to look harmless and failing if the alarm pinching his face was any indication. Or maybe it was Sebille's RBF, resting barracuda face, over my shoulder that was making him tense. Whatever it was, the man looked like he might pee his pants if he had any. "We have a big problem and we need your help."

One thick, black brow lifted. "Oh? And you believe this is a new thing? You having a problem?"

I frowned at him. "No, but..."

Out of the corner of my eye, I saw Sebille pretending to light a match and drop it on him.

Some of the color left Osvald's ruddy face. "What's the problem?"

I told him about the ancient black and white television, even stepping aside to show him its effects.

He paled another couple of shades when he saw the giant, colorless area around it. "Oh my."

"Yeah," I said, staring at it with what I was sure was a worried gaze. "And three of my friends were sucked into that thing. I need to know how to get them out."

Osvald's head shook back and forth on the air. "I'm very sorry for your loss, Keeper. But you cannot retrieve your friends. They are lost in that world now."

He didn't seem sorry at all. In fact, I saw a glimmer of satisfaction in his black eyes.

I gritted my teeth against the desire to screech at him, my hand fisting at my sides. It probably wouldn't do to punch the disembodied head into the wall behind the desk.

It might leave a greasy mark on the paint.

"Try again, Professor," Sebille said.

His black gaze rolled toward my assistant and widened. I turned to find her holding a roiling ball of green energy in her palm. He shook his head. "I can't help you..."

The ball of energy grew.

Osvald made a small sound of fear and pointed his nose toward the book, clearly intending to *book* it out of there.

I placed a hand over Sebille's energy, extinguishing it. Taking a deep breath, I decided to appeal to his ego. "Please, Doctor Osvald. Nobody knows more about this kind of thing than you do. Can't you help us?"

He reluctantly slid his gaze from Sebille and stared at me for a long moment, his heavy, cracked lips still compressed into an unhappy line. Finally, he sighed.

"Chapter Five," he intoned in a colorless voice. The pages of the book on the desk flipped forward to the chapter he'd requested, falling still as a large, ornate number five appeared on top of the page.

Osvald directed his attention downward, spinning to see the book better. "Time and reality-altering artifacts are singularly dangerous due to their determined focus," he read. "The goal of this type of artifact is to remake the Universe in the image of that which they embrace. All else falls to the wayside. Any attempt to interrupt the flow of their invasive magic is quickly and thoroughly preempted, and the 'attacker' dispatched in a suitable way."

"Dispatched?" I squeaked, my stomach churning with acid.

Osvald's greasy head nodded. "In this case, I believe you'd be flung into the abyss without a means of returning. But there are always more fatal options."

"But who, or what would be policing the magic?" Sebille asked, frowning.

Osvald shrugged his dense black eyebrows. "That depends on the reality at the forefront when the victims were tugged inside."

My memory replayed the whistling theme song, and I cringed. "Andrew of Mayberry. I have a couple of artifacts from that show."

Osvald's gaze widened. "You do? That might help if you decide to go inside."

"Inside?" I asked, dread turning my palms sweaty. "What do you mean?"

"It's the only chance you'll have, Keeper. If you want to help your friends and stop this artifact from spreading its poison everywhere. You're going to have to immerse yourself into the world of Andrew of Mayberry and find a way to shut it down. From the inside."

3

BURN THE THREAT INTO OBLIVION

"I can't believe none of these books can tell us how to stop one of these artifacts," I exclaimed, shoving a long strand of brown hair behind my ears in a sign of my growing frustration.

Rustin sat back and ran a hand over his face. "What I got from that reference book I read was that this type of artifact is rare. Information on dealing with it is very limited. Only two Keepers have dealt with a time and reality morphing artifact."

Hope rose in my chest. "I assume they defeated their artifacts since the world isn't black and white, and I don't hear a whistling soundtrack in the background."

Sebille, Rustin, and I were sitting around Shakespeare's desk, discussing what Rustin had learned in *Magical Objects to Avoid at all Costs*. Which wasn't much. For such an extensive magical reference book, there apparently hadn't been much information on a black and white television artifact from the nineteen sixties.

Rustin sighed. "I'm not sure you could classify it as defeating them."

"What do you mean?" Sebille asked.

The ghost witch threw me a quick, worried glance. "The Keepers both sacrificed themselves to stop the artifacts from spreading."

My pulse shot skyward. "Sacrificed themselves? How?"

He stared down at the open books littering the desk. Finally, he sighed. "Apparently, if you overload the system, the artifact blows up."

I shook my head. "Not an option. Not until I get the kids out of there."

Rustin's lips twitched at my calling Mr. Wicked, Mr. Slimy, and Hobs "the kids".

"How did they overload the system?" Sebille asked.

"It doesn't matter because it's not happening," I said.

Sebille motioned for me to hush. "If we're going to defeat this thing and get them back, we need as much knowledge as possible, Naida."

"No. She's right," Rustin said, frowning. "We're not going to be able to recreate their methods. First of all, we'd need a second time and reality-altering artifact."

"A second one?" Curiosity had me asking. "Why?"

"The Keepers placed the two objects within the same sphere and they battled each other for control of the environment."

That sounded promising.

"Okay," Sebille said. "We can work with that."

Rustin shook his head. "You don't understand. These objects have natural self-protective instincts. If they find themselves in a hostile environment, they attack everything within their sphere. The destruction could encompass all of Croakies." He fixed me with a sad expression. "The only way it will work is if someone who has control over artifacts holds them in place and under their control long enough for their conflicting drives to terminate them both. Those Keepers stood between the two artifacts and forced them to stay in proximity until they were destroyed. And when they went, the Keepers were extinguished with them."

Despair tightened my chest. Not at the idea of being extinguished, though that was certainly terrifying. I was more concerned over the lack of a rescue option for Wicked and gang in that scenario.

I looked around the library. I also didn't want to risk losing everything to stop the artifact.

"What about Dugan McDonald?" I asked the ghost witch.

"What about him?" Rustin asked on a frown.

"The artifact poisoned his home. According to Grym, it's still poisoning it even though he's gone. Does that mean the effects will keep spreading until we find some way to stop it?"

"From what I read in this," He placed a hand over the thick, leather-bound reference book, "The spread stops when the artifact is extinguished."

"What about the de-coloration that's already there?" Sebille asked. "Is it reversible?"

"I just don't know," Rustin said. "But that's a problem for another day. We need to stop the spread first."

I hugged myself feeling cold and scared.

"I wonder why this artifact never triggered at Theo's place," Rustin mused.

I shrugged. "Probably because of his home artifact. A giant's home artifact is naturally superior against any incoming artifact. It's first choice is to pull the new artifact into the group, make it part of the main artifact, but if an artifact refuses to join, it's cauterized away from the rest. Given its power-hungry ways, I'm guessing the TV artifact would have eventually won over the rest, but Theo has a very active home artifact. It would have taken a while for the new artifact to gain control."

We sat in silence for a beat, thinking over what we knew. It wasn't much. Finally, I sighed. "Professor Osvald said I needed to go inside to stop the artifact, but he couldn't tell me if it was possible." I lifted my gaze to Rustin, tears burning my lids. "I have to try to save them, Rustin. And Mr. McDonald too," I said. "If I can stop the artifact while I'm inside, then all the better. If not...then we'll try it your way."

Rustin's handsome face darkened. He shoved his wire-rimmed glasses up his nose with a jerky motion. "It's not *my* way, Naida. It's just all I've found." He shrugged, clearly trying to reach for calm. "I don't want you to die."

I reached over and grabbed his hand, giving it a slightly desperate squeeze. "I don't want to die either," I told him. "We'll find another way."

"You'd need to find another time and reality changing artifact anyway," he said, sounding almost relieved. "You'll never find one. They're rare."

Sebille and I shared a look. I knew what she was thinking because I was thinking the same thing. We had another such artifact in the library, though if I'd known how dangerous it was, I'd have already put it into the toxic magic vault.

Sebille gave me a little nod and stood. "I'll go take care of it."

Watching her walk away to grab the record player that sucked the listener into the time and place of whatever song was playing, I felt my mind go still. I knew what I had to do, and I was resolved to do it.

"This is a rescue mission first," I told Rustin. "Then we'll deal with the rest."

The rest was probably going to include my death. I really didn't want to focus on that at the moment. The most important thing was the rescue.

Rustin just shook his head, determinedly avoiding my gaze.

A firm knock sounded on the dividing door and I flinched.

Rustin reached out and clasped my hand. "I'll deal with it."

I expelled a relieved breath. "Thanks. If it's something you can't answer, tell them I'll be with them in a few minutes. I just need..." I sighed, and he nodded.

"Whoever it is, I'll put them off."

I rested my head on my arms and expelled a long breath, fighting not to give in to the worry and despair filling me. My eyes fell on the large, manilla envelope I'd shoved to the back of the desk several days earlier.

It was the package from Archibald Pudsnecker. Archie was the Sorcerer of the Voids we'd worked with when Croakies had been overrun by monsters. He'd helped me find the breach in the abyss that was letting the monsters through. And he'd seemed very determined for me to read the contents of the envelope. I tugged it closer, my fingers sliding it open before my brain had time to wonder if it was a good idea, given everything that was going on.

I pulled out a thin sheaf of papers covered in a

handwritten scrawl that sparked a memory some-where deep inside.

I frowned. I'd been expecting information about Archie's books. That had been how he'd approached me. Offering himself for a book signing at Croakies. I'd later learned that the book signing thing had been a ruse. But somehow, I'd convinced myself that was what was in the packet.

As I started reading the long, long letter clutched between my fingers, I quickly learned the missive was far from a proposal to sign books.

Dear Naida,

I know this letter will come as a surprise to you... perhaps even a shock. But if you've received it now, then it's time for you to know about your past. First, let me tell you that I'm very sorry to have left you on your own for this long. It was a cruelty, yes. But a necessary one.

I've done...things...I'm not proud of. I've brought danger down on my own head, and I'd only hoped to spare you from my poor choices. To do that, I had to remove myself from your life. Of all the things plaguing my existence, that is the thing that takes the largest chunk from my heart. Don't blame Archie. He did the best he could. If he was unequal to the task, that is not his fault. He simply didn't understand. That too was my fault...

"Naida?"

I jumped, so immersed in the strange letter that I'd lost track of everything outside the tight, tidy script on the page. I shoved the pages back into the envelope and looked up at Sebille, trying to make my expression as neutral as possible. "What?"

She narrowed her astounding green gaze on me. "Are you okay? You look like you've seen a ghost."

If she only knew.

I nodded quickly. Too quickly. And forced a smile that felt tight on my cheeks. "I'm fine. Well, not fine, but coping." I frowned. "Is it safe?"

She blinked as if trying to change tracks, and then her expression cleared as she caught my meaning. "The record player is locked in the vault." She shook her head. "I can't believe we had that out and just sitting around." There was accusation in her words, a quiet bitterness I knew was pointed at me. I was a terrible Keeper of the Artifacts. I knew less than nothing about my job. And I was sick of feeling guilty about that.

Something had to change.

If I survived the next couple of days, I was going to do as Archie had suggested and recall the Keeper who'd trained me. She'd done a terrible job and needed to fix the holes in my knowledge before I lost everyone I cared about. But there was nothing I could do about my inadequacies at the moment. All I could do was try to fix the immediate issue. "I don't understand why I couldn't *feel* how dangerous it was."

Even with my inadequacies, I'd fully embraced

my KoA magics. I could feel the role and placement of every object within the artifact library. I'd grown exponentially in my power. But both the television and the record player had masked themselves from me.

Not good.

Sebille shrugged. "It must be something about their particular type of energy."

"I need to get them out of there, Sebille. That's all that matters now." Tears burned my eyes.

She stared at me for a long moment. There was sadness in her gaze, even while her stiff posture seemed to project anger toward me. "I can ask mother."

Sebille's mother was Queen of the Fae in Enchanted. She was a powerful supernormal with the ability to read and decipher all types of magic energy. She'd only recently returned to my friend Lea's greenhouse where the Fae were currently living. She'd come back from a meeting of the magic council in Illusion City, where she'd petitioned for the right to relocate to the primordial forest.

A fact that might have something to do with the sadness in Sebille's usually hostile gaze.

"Has she decided what she's going to do?" I asked the sprite in a gentle voice.

Sebille shook her head. "She won't say anything about her meetings. All she says is that my brothers miss me."

Sebille had several brothers and one sister living in the primordial forest. It was one of the reasons Queen Sindra was considering the move. Though, I knew from Sebille that her younger sister, Salina, drove the queen crazy, and I suspected she and Sebille didn't get along either since Sebille rarely mentioned her.

I nodded. "I'm praying to the goddess every single day that she decides to stay here."

Sebille nodded, her gaze dropping from mine.

I could almost read her mind. She didn't want me to see how worried she was about it. Pity for my assistant tightened my chest. I quickly extinguished it. She wouldn't thank me for feeling pity. She was far more likely to smack me upside the head for it. "Yes. Call her. Please? Hopefully, she can tell me how to get them back."

"Us," Sebille said, glowering at me.

"Huh?"

"Whatever needs doing, I'm helping you. You can't do this alone."

I didn't like the idea of endangering Sebille too. I secretly told myself I'd find a way to go without her. But I only nodded. If she knew what I was thinking, she'd smack me again for having the thought.

Her gaze narrowed suspiciously as if she could read my mind, Sebille finally turned away and headed for the communication mirror. A moment later, I heard her talking to her mother.

My gaze slid to the yellow envelope, my fingers creeping over to touch the edge. Instinctively, I knew the words inside would change my life forever. They'd turn everything I knew on its head and leave me feeling even more bereft than I already did.

A sudden, raging fear tightened beneath my ribs. I wanted to burn the envelope to ash and never read what was inside. Instead, I shoved it to the back of the desk and covered it with the slowly dwindling pile of artifact orders.

I couldn't allow myself to get distracted in that way. Not now. Maybe not ever.

If I was smart, I'd do what my instincts told me to do. And burn the threat into oblivion.

4

NAIDA DEAR, THIS IS BAD

Queen Sindra circled the monotone area, taking care to stay well out of reach of the destructive magics. Beside her, as she worked, was another Fae, whose larger size and straight dark hair told me he was an elf. The elf's silver and black wings, more like a moth's than a butterfly's were also a clear sign of his magical designation. While Queen Sindra wove a netting of light green magic upon the air, the elf inserted silvery motes of energy within the Queen's power, forming a wavering line that rose and fell in seemingly random fashion through the web.

Like magical reinforcement.

When the ends of the silver energies met each other, closing the circle, the two Fae flew back to where Sebille, Rustin, and I were waiting, near the staircase leading to my apartment.

Sindra's beautiful, butterfly-like wings throbbed so quickly on the air that all I could see was a soft blur of pink, purple, and neon green. She smiled at Sebille, who hadn't been in the room when the queen had arrived. "Daughter. How do you fare?"

Sebille winced only slightly. She hated using the overly formal language of the Fae Court, but she'd relaxed her disdain over the last few months. Probably because she'd watched her people be nearly extinguished by Jacob Quilleran, in addition to the more recent threat of losing her mother's regular presence in her life. "I'm fine, Mother. You look well."

The pleasantries complete, Queen Sindra inclined her chin and looked to me. "I'm certain I don't need to tell you, Naida dear, this is bad."

I frowned, nodding. "We've been studying the problem. We know our choices are limited."

"I surrounded the artifact with energy that stimulated it into engaging in order to try to find a weak spot. We were unable to find one. But, as I worked, Adolfo was analyzing the energy," she told us. "Dolfo, please tell the Keeper what you've found."

The handsome elf buzzed forward, bowing slightly to Sebille before straightening to look me in the eye. His blue eyes were so dark they looked black in his tiny face, and the heavy black uniform of the Queen's guards only strengthened that effect. With his black and silver wings, pale skin, black hair, and angular slash of black brows, he looked as if the artifact had caught him up and drained him of color.

In a good way.

"Keeper. Princess. It's an honor to be of service."

Sebille nodded stiffly and I felt a random urge to give her a hug. She was handling the whole *Princess* thing very well.

"Thank you for your help, Adolfo," I told the handsome elf.

"As the Queen has already informed you, I infused her protective web with analytical magics. While it is in place, my magic will continually read the energy flowing from the artifact, looking for the optimum time for you to insert yourself into the magical footprint."

"We've been told we can't affect the magical footprint of this artifact," I said.

"That is technically true," Adolfo said. "But as in all things magical, there is a back door."

"Explain," Sebille ordered.

"You cannot disrupt the energy of this artifact. You cannot damage the magics. If you try, you will be attacked. But you might be able to insert yourself if you become invisible to the protections within it."

"What Adolfo is trying to say in a diplomatic fashion," Queen Sindra said with a fond look toward her daughter, "Is that you can be accepted as part of the magic. But you cannot barge into it as a hostile, foreign entity."

"What does that mean in practical terms?" Rustin asked, frowning.

Sindra shrugged. "You must make yourself look like the target entity. You must assimilate rather than violate the magical footprint."

"What does that mean, though? We can't leech the color from ourselves," I said.

"You won't need to," Adolfo said. "The magic will do that for you. But you must look like the world you are targeting. You must be dressed as they would dress, embrace the culture. If you have props tied to that world, it will help immeasurably."

I thought of the Andrew of Mayberry plates I had, which constantly refilled with home cooking once the food was consumed. "I have two things that would work there."

"You must leave behind the things of this world," Sindra warned. "A single item from this world will alert the energy of your 'otherness', and it will be the death of you."

Nodding my understanding, I swallowed hard. A sudden, true understanding of how dangerous the insertion would be squeezed cold fingers around my heart.

I looked at Adolfo. "Your analytical energy will tell us when it's safe to go inside?"

He nodded.

"Will we get any warning?" Rustin asked. "Time to prepare?"

"Not much," Adolfo said, his expression filled with apology. "I recommend you ready yourselves to go at any time."

Black and white bat boogers! I thought in despair. I had to walk around in a flowered dress with an apron and a plate of pie in my hand? Even given the pure entertainment of watching Sebille try to look retro, life was going to be bleak indeed.

S ebille stood behind the sales counter at Croakies, the fringed tip of her fire-engine red braid in her hand, and her eyes nearly crossed from looking at it.

"What?" I asked, irritation spiking. The sprite had refused to dress in the manner required to enter the world of Andrew of Mayberry at a moment's notice. And she hadn't hidden her smile when she'd looked at me. Instead, as I sat with the store's financial records spread out in front of me, she'd done nothing but stare at her split ends. It was especially annoying knowing that sprites didn't get split ends. I knew I was being cranky because of my worry over Wicked and gang. I was also feeling guilty that I'd had to call Mrs. Foxladle and cancel book club again. But the sprite was getting on my last nerve.

"Stop staring at your hair and come help me with these books."

She rolled her eyes. "What are you doing with them, anyway? We don't have to get them to the accountant for another three weeks."

"I want to make sure everything's in order now, just in case the worst happens." The thought filled my eyes with tears. If the worst did happen, I'd have lost everything and everyone I loved. And aside from the idea of losing Sebille, Wicked, Slimy, and Hobs, the second worst part was that I had nobody to leave Croakies to. I had no living family that I knew of. The closest I had to an advisor was a man I barely knew. Still, I planned to pen a letter to Archibald Pudsnecker with instructions on how I wanted Croakies dispersed.

I scanned a look toward the dividing door, knowing I should finish reading the letter that Archie had sent me. Maybe there was more information on what had happened to my mother.

I also wanted to talk to Archie about why he'd had the letter in the first place. He hadn't admitted to being a relative or even a friend of my parents. Yet he'd been mentioned in the letter. What was he to me?

It was interesting that he was a sorcerer. That would imply some connection to me since the world of sorcery was relatively small compared to some of the other magical designations.

"I wasn't staring at my hair," Sebille groused as she flopped into the chair across from me. "Well, technically I was, but I was just wondering what it would look like black. I've always had red hair. I can't imagine it black, can you? I mean your hair is just brown. It won't be much of a change. But mine..."

I knew Sebille's seemingly unimportant worry was just her way of trying to accept what we were about to do. As long as I'd known her, she'd seemed totally unconcerned with how she looked. In fact, with her outrageous outfits, she'd seemed to actively defy anyone to judge her appearance.

"It could turn white, you know," I told her, feeling only a little guilty for teasing her since she'd had no compunction against teasing me. "Or gray."

Her eyes went wide. "Gray?"

My lips twitched, giving me away. "It will only be temporary," I told her. "As soon as we come home, it will turn red again." I hoped.

Besides, I told myself, I had no intention of letting her come with me. It was just too dangerous. When Adolfo told me, and only me, according to my instructions to him before he left, that it was time, I planned to insert myself into the artifact alone.

Then why, you're probably wondering, am I insisting that Sebille go retro with me? That's simple. I'd pay money to see Sebille clad in the mid-calf-length flowered dress and boring black pumps that I was reluctantly wearing.

Especially with a tidy white apron.

I'd give six inches of my long, curly and apparently boring brown hair to see that.

Yes, I would.

"Rustin called," the sprite told me. "He said he found a great retro clothing store. He's bringing us stuff." She grimaced.

"That's good," I told her, trying to focus on the books. I was having trouble reconciling the birdseed expenditures with the total expenses figure. I was sure I'd spent more than the figure in the books. But something had been erased in the column for the final amounts. "Did you change this number here?" I pointed to the erasure.

Sebille shook her head. "No. What is it?"

The bell on the exterior door jangled softly, announcing the arrival of a customer. Only it wasn't a customer. It was Grym.

Sebille and I stared at him a long moment, our eyes slowly growing to the size of golf balls.

He glared back at us, all but daring us to comment on the way he looked.

"Um," I said.

Sebille giggled, drawing an even darker glower from the cop.

"It was all I could find that would fit," he said, glancing down at the pants that were no less than three inches too short.

"Those fit, huh?" I asked, clearing my throat to hide the giggle dancing on my tonsils.

"Better than the other clothes I've tried," he said, grimacing. He ran thick fingers beneath the ugly suspenders that were ostensibly keeping his too-tight, too-short pants on his hips. "These things pinch."

I rolled my lips together, pressing them tight against the smile burning to be released. "I, um, like the hair."

He reached up and ran a hand over the ruthlessly slicked mahogany strands. I wondered if his fingers came away coated in grease. "It's not bad, huh?"

"Are those bowling shoes?" Sebille asked, finally giving up and snorting out a laugh.

His caramel gaze scoured her in acid. "They're the closest thing I could find to saddle shoes."

Against my best intentions, the laugh I'd been trying to hold back erupted. "They're very, saddle-ee."

Grym sighed. "I'll feel better when we get this trip behind us."

I hadn't intended for the cop to join me in world hopping. I hadn't intended for anyone to join me. But it seemed he had other ideas. "Look, Grym..."

He held up a blocky hand. "Don't waste your breath, Naida. I'm coming. If we don't fix this, McDonald's house is going to continue to lose color, the poison spreading until it starts leaching out onto the lawn and onward from there. It's my job to find the man and to stop the spread of this toxic magic. I want to protect Enchanted."

I could understand his feelings because I shared them. Rather than argue with him, I simply nodded. I'd just have to sneak away from him too.

I bit back a sigh. The whole thing was getting too complex. Thinking about that, along with my lost friends and the letter waiting for me in the library, was too depressing. So I changed the subject. "Still no sign of McDonald, huh?"

Grym shook his head. "He's got to be inside that thing."

I had a thought that was worrying. "We don't know what show he was watching when he was pulled inside. What if he was watching something other than Andrew of Mayberry?" As I asked the question, my stomach twisted with alarm. I had no idea how to find my friends and stop the artifact in *one* world. There was no way I'd be able to navigate two worlds and stop the artifact all by myself. I chewed my bottom lip.

A chime sounded from inside the artifact library. Sebille and I shared a look. It was the communicating mirror.

"Adolfo?" I asked,

She shrugged. "I'll go see what he wants."

Grym tugged out his cell. "I'll call Rustin and tell him he needs to get back here."

I opened my mouth to tell him not to bother,

knowing I was going on a solo mission. But I couldn't think of a way to say it without cluing Grym in on what I planned.

Bristly bear buttocks! Why was nothing ever simple?

Sebille slammed the dividing door and stomped over to us. I'd have thought she was angry about something, except that was pretty much how she always walked in her ill-fitting Wicked Witch of the West shoes. "He said something's changing and we're to be ready. It's close."

My chest tightened. I glanced toward the door, knowing I needed to find a way to get to the artifact without their knowing. Maybe I could throw a magical lock on the dividing door so they couldn't follow me inside.

"I'm just going to go to the back..."

I never got a chance to finish that sentence. The front door opened again, and a familiar yet totally unfamiliar face and form came through.

All of our mouths dropped open as Lea bounced into the store, a bright smile on her face.

Hex trotted in behind her, tail snapping with emotion.

"Erg..." Sebille burbled nonsensically.

Lea laughed gaily, clapping her hands. "Isn't it blustery?"

The slang term was i*cy*, but Lea regularly butchered it.

She stood before us in a button-up white blouse that fit her more tightly than her usual garb, covered by a thin pink cardigan that came to the middle of her forearms and just below her waist. Her bottom half was covered in a pink...poodle...skirt that flared away from her rounded hips to an alarming width. I call it a poodle skirt because there was an honest-to-goddess poodle on the front. The decorative dog was formed from fabric and beading, a curving line of beads leading from the fabric dog collar like a leash. The end of the leash wrapped around the skirt and disappeared somewhere behind Lea.

White socks were folded at her ankles, and her feet were covered in flat shoes with rounded toes and straps across the top. Her long, light-brown hair was twisted up into a high ponytail, the thick pony glossy and softly curled on the ends. Her buoyant 'do bounced around her head when she moved, looking manically happy like she appeared to be.

"Isn't it great?" Lea asked.

It was definitely something. I wasn't sure great was the word I was reaching for. I settled for a non-committal sound. "Hmm."

My friend seemed satisfied with that.

I fixed a scolding look on her. "You're not coming."

Her smile died. "Yes, I am."

"Lea..." I whined.

She shook her head, sending the ponytail into

spasms of delight. "I want to help. Hex can find Wicked, simplifying the search, and I can help you figure out how to stop that thing from whatever it's doing."

I stared at her for a long moment, putting all of my unhappiness into my gaze. Her well-shaped lips tightened into a hard, determined line and I knew I was lost. I'd never talk her out of coming along. There was possibly only one person who was more stubborn than Sebille or me, and that was Lea.

I expelled a frustrated breath, giving in less than gracefully. "Fine!"

Lea's grin immediately returned. I envied her that emotional resiliency. I'd suffer under a cloud of residual crankiness for at least an hour.

"We just got the word," Sebille told my friend the witch. "We're to get prepared. Something's changing in the magic."

Lea nodded. "Good. The sooner we get this over with, the better."

I didn't respond. Instead, I turned on my heel and stalked toward the dividing door. I wasn't sure where I was going or what I would do once I got there. I only knew I needed to put some space between me and all my "helpful" friends, who were probably going to die right along with me.

That was not what I'd planned at all.

Not even close.

DISAPPEARING INTO MIST

Unfortunately, I didn't make it to the back. The front door opened again, and Rustin walked into Croakies. I perused the ghost witch with a critical and twitching eye. I tried rubbing the eye, but it just kept twitching. "Um."

Lea reached over and tugged on his red and white polka-dotted bow tie. "I think he looks very handsome," she said.

Her statement put me immediately on the defensive as Rustin lifted a dark eyebrow in silent accusation. "I'm not saying he doesn't look handsome..."

Rustin's second brow arched up to join the first and I realized I'd stepped out of the sucking mud into quicksand. I sighed. "I'm just not sure you're in the right decade." Or century. The pants he was wearing had a waistline somewhere up around his nipples and flared into twin mermaid fins down by his ankles. "What are those pants, anyway?"

He grinned. "Bellbottoms. Cool, huh?"

"Yeah," I coughed as my throat caught on the word. "Downright blizzardy."

Lea's grin widened. I was pretty sure she was filing the non-word into her cool slang file to be misused later.

I shook off my concern. I mean, it wasn't like I could do anything about the ruffly shirt that looked as if he could wear it to sail the seven seas with Sewer Beak the parrot on his shoulder, the weird tie, or the even weirder pants. But the shoes...

I narrowed my gaze on the brown and white monstrosities. "Are those giant baby shoes?"

Sebille snorted, covering her mouth with a hand as Rustin glared over at her. "I'll have you know these were the height of fashion."

"When?" Sebille asked, quite reasonably I thought.

Rustin's mouth opened and then closed. He shrugged. "I'm pretty sure I'm in the right century. Andrew of Mayberry will just have to deal with it."

"He's going to think the circus is in town," I mumbled, looking around at my hapless group of merry weirdos.

Sebille, who still hadn't changed out of her signature sprite costume, shook her head. "We're doomed."

"We'll be in and out before they even have time to notice our clothes," Grym said.

"Where's Sadie?" Lea asked the ghost witch.

He frowned. "I sent her to Maude. She can't go into the artifact. If it strips her colors, she'll lose all of her energy. We aren't sure what that would do to her. Maude believed it might kill her."

Maude Quilleran was Rustin's cousin and a young but very powerful witch. She was the one who'd given the little dragon to the ghost witch, and I knew she'd take good care of her.

"Speaking of Maude," I said, narrowing my gaze on the ghost witch, "You can't come with us. You haven't mastered your dual nature yet. What if you burst into...whatever you are in your second form... in the middle of this adventure? That would just about blow the lid off of anything we were trying to do."

When Rustin had been cursed into Slimy by his Uncle Jacob Quilleran, his aunt Madeline and his cousin Maude had used their prodigious magical abilities to find a way for him to regain his body. They'd come up with giving him a dual form, one of which was him and one was a supernormal form which nobody had yet seen.

Rustin narrowed his gaze right back at me. "I've been working on my control. I'll be fine."

"What's the longest you've kept your current form," I asked, "I mean, minus the baby shoes?"

Sebille tittered gleefully.

"Two days," he responded, his expression cocky. "Don't worry about me, I'll be fine, Naida. We aren't going to be gone longer than that."

I clamped my lips shut, a wave of new worry hitting me as I added concern about Rustin to the rest of the mess. The ever-growing morass of worries only served to remind me just how dangerous our journey was going to be.

The communicating mirror dinged a warning. I hurried into the library as the smoky-gray of the empty glass was replaced in the center by a quickly enlarging dot of vibrant green. When the connection had opened completely, the vivid hues of Lea's greenhouse filled the background. Adolfo hovered in the foreground, his black and gray wings buzzing softly as he held himself aloft. His gaze slid immediately to Lea and her cheeks went pink.

"Hello, Lea?"

A giggle burst from my best friend's lips.

A giggle!

I narrowed my gaze on them. Had they been up to some hanky type panky behind my back? Or in front of my front...since I was generally clueless about what was going on around me most of the time? "Do you have news?" I asked the overly friendly elf.

His smile turned upside down before he yanked his gaze from Lea. If I didn't know better,

I'd think the elf didn't want the witch to come with.

On that, at least, we could agree.

"Yes. The magic is coalescing. You will soon see a series of events occur." He buzzed closer, his tiny form taking up more of the mirrored surface. "Pay careful attention. You must do exactly what I say, exactly when I say to do it."

We all nodded as if our heads were connected by a single string.

"First, the artifact will turn itself on."

We all looked toward the ancient TV, whose screen had gone dark sometime after the color leeching had begun.

"At first, it will be only static. Like electric snow."

"Okay," I said, my tone impatient.

Adolfo sent me a reproachful glance. "The artifact will stay in that state for a short time and then an entertainment artifact will come on. I believe you refer to it as a television show. That is when you can enter the colorless sphere." He frowned. "It's important for you to understand, that sphere represents the live zone. The artifact can affect your actions anywhere inside that sphere."

He waited for us to nod before going on.

"It will stay live almost indefinitely once it's activated. But after you've entered the sphere, you will have precisely two minutes before you are drawn inexorably inside. There's no turning back once it begins to pull you in."

I wiped my suddenly sweating palms over my ugly flowered dress. "There's nothing we can do once we're in the live zone?"

He turned a worried glance on me. "At the two-minute mark you will lose the ability to affect anything."

"Do you know anything about how we will find our friends once inside?" Sebille asked.

Adolfo gave a start and performed a quick bow on the air. "My apologies, Princess. I failed to greet you properly."

Sebille rolled her eyes. "Answer my question, please."

"Unfortunately, I do not. Nor can I or the queen assist you in stopping the artifact. All I can do is read the action segmentation in the magical signature."

"You can't give us anything?" Lea asked, her voice soft, almost pleading.

Adolfo went very still, brows lowering over his dark eyes. "I cannot give you specifics for this particular artifact. But I do know this. In each time and reality affecting artifact, there is a heart that beats to protect the artifact. If you extinguish that beating heart, you will be able to defeat the artifact. Though the means of defeating it are unknown."

"May the goddess be with you on your journey."

Adolfo inclined his dark head and, with a final, worried glance toward Lea, severed the connection, and the mirror went dark.

"Great," Sebille groused. "All we have to help us is a bad riddle."

Lea frowned. "That's not fair, Sebille. He was only trying to help."

The sprite shook her head. "I'm going to go make tea…"

The ancient television kicked on. The small, square screen filled with the loud sound of electronic static.

We all shared a look.

"Well, this is it," I said, my voice breaking on the last word.

Grym reached out and clasped my hand, giving it a reassuring squeeze. "We're going to find them, Naida."

I nodded, my eyes suddenly burning with tears. "Look, you guys, I really don't want…"

"Zip it," sayeth the sprite. "We're coming. You can't stop us."

I gathered myself up and glared at them. "I'm the Keeper. This is my job. None of you should come. It could be dangerous and…" My stern tone was all but obliterated under the tears sliding down my cheeks. "I can't lose you all too."

"We're coming, Naida," Rustin said, giving me a

sad smile. "We don't want to lose you or the trouble-some trio either."

"Besides," said Sebille, "You're not the boss of me."

I snorted out a laugh before I narrowed my gaze on her. "Actually, sprite, I *am* the boss of you." I grabbed the never-ending slice of pie artifact off Shakespeare's desk. It was one of two Andrew of Mayberry artifacts I had. I hadn't been able to find the never-ending plate of chicken dinner artifact. I was pretty sure Hobs had that tucked away in his hidey-hole.

"Not really," Sebille responded. "I just let you think you are."

Grym chuckled and I glared over at him. But I didn't try to argue the point. Everybody in the room knew she was right.

The static sound abruptly dropped away under the familiar sound of that whistling theme song.

I closed my eyes and took a deep breath.

It was time.

I turned to my friends with a plea in my gaze, determined to try one more time to talk them out of entering the artifact. I blinked in surprise as I saw Sebille step into the monochrome sphere, Rustin right behind her.

Lea and Hex were already there. Hex looked no different except for her eyes which were a nondescript dark gray. Lea's poodle was gray, her skirt black. And her pretty blue eyes had turned a pale gray.

With a whoosh of silvery magic, Sebille's fiery hair dulled under the color-stripping energy, followed by her neon green dress and red and black striped stockings. Lastly, I watched her Wicked Witch of the West shoes go dull, fading to charcoal gray.

When I tore my gaze away from my assistant, I was shocked to see that Rustin had also bleached to grays and blacks, his handsome face looking a sickly gray. With his normal black hair, it was slightly less startling than Sebille's transformation had been, but it was disturbing enough to make it hard to breathe.

Grym offered me his hand. I glanced up at him, his caramel gaze focusing a question in my direction. "Ready?" he asked.

I took a deep breath and nodded. Taking hold of his warm hand, I stepped over the curved line into a monochrome world.

The silvery magic tickled against my skin as it washed over me. As it sifted away, I looked down to find my hands white and my clothing shades of black and gray. Beside me, Grym chuckled softly. I turned to find him examining his hands and arms. That was when I realized the new color scheme was very close to his color in gargoyle form.

He lifted a black gaze to me, and it made me

shiver. Even as a gargoyle, Grym's gaze would normally be a warm golden brown. Without even that little bit of color, the change felt dangerously permanent.

"We should all cross together," Rustin said, "So we don't get separated inside."

I felt my eyes go wide. I hadn't even considered that. He was right. It would be easy for us to be shunted off to different black and white television shows. Though the familiar characters of Andrew of Mayberry made me believe the show could be the only destination.

Moving together, we grabbed each other's hands and, with a final look and a nod, we stepped close to the artifact as a united front.

For a moment, nothing happened. In fact, it went on for long enough that I frowned, starting to worry that our attempt to crash the 1960s would fail.

But then I felt a strange tingling in my lower extremities. By the time I realized something was happening and glanced down, my legs were gone up to my knees.

Well, not gone, precisely. More like fractured into millions of tiny, sparkling motes dancing around beneath me in a vaguely leg-shaped form.

The tingling spread so quickly I barely had time to panic as my entire body was consumed into tiny pieces of light. As the energy reached my head, I opened my mouth to scream, and the sound never emerged. With a flash of near-painful electrical energy, I became air. My very last terrorized thought clung to the emptiness for a split second and then dissipated in a flash.

Disappearing into mist.

6

IF YOU CAIN'T SWIM, WHAT WAS YOU
DOIN' IN THAT POND?

S ound returned first, a cacophony of terrified screaming, that grew gradually louder as light and movement re-entered the picture.

That was when I realized I was falling.

I mentally flailed my arms, only to recognize I had no arms. A beat later they were back, but I had no legs to catch myself as I saw the grainy, taupe-ish landscape far below rushing up to meet me.

The sensation of being totally out of control was probably what had multiple screams reverberating across the countryside. In a total reverse to how my body had turned into television snow, it quickly reassembled itself as I fell.

By the time I reached the colorless grass beside the gray and silvery pond, I was fully formed again. I wish I could say that helped when I landed. It didn't cushion the fall. Not one little bit. And I slammed into the hard, dusty ground with the force of a freight train smacking a brick wall.

The plate filled with never-ending pie landed on my stomach, unharmed and not even dusty.

Stupid pie. If I got out of the current mess, I was never eating pie again. I placed the plate next to me and lay there a moment, trying to catch my breath.

I'd landed hard enough to knock all the wind out of my lungs, slicing off the warbling scream I hadn't even realized until that moment had been tearing the silent fabric of the pastoral spot into shreds.

I lay there, a melodic and familiar whistling playing across my inner ears, and tried to take inventory of all my battered parts.

Two more heavy thumps sent dust into the air around me. The landings were followed by soft groans that mirrored my own.

A distant splash brought my gaze snapping open as my brain finally kicked in. Somebody had literally splash-landed into the small but picturesque pond that was only a few yards away.

I scanned the mounds of monochrome flesh around me. Who was missing? "Where's Lea?" I groaned. "And Grym," I added, shoving painfully to my feet.

"Hey!" a deep voice called out.

I turned to find Grym treading water pretty far out on the pond.

"Hey!" he screamed again. "I can't..." His dark

head disappeared beneath the silvered surface of the water, his flailing hands the last to disappear. With a start, I realized what he'd been about to say.

I took off running, ignoring the stiffness of my joints and the sharp slicing of residual pain from my fall. "Grym's in trouble," I yelled to Sebille and Rustin. I spotted a small rowboat on the shore and veered in that direction.

Something niggled in my mind about that tidy looking boat, but I was too worried about Grym to try to lock the thought down. The gargoyle was splashing around in the water, sending a prodigious amount of liquid into the air around him as he struggled to keep his head above the surface.

Rustin reached the boat before I did and started shoving it toward the pond. He glanced at me. "You'd better stay here. I'm not sure how much weight this thing can hold, and Grym's heavy."

I bit back an argument, giving the flat back of the small boat a shove that I hoped would send it well out into the pond.

"Isn't that the boat from episode two?" Sebille asked.

I frowned, wondering if I should tease her for having watched the shows. I settled for a quick glance in her direction to arch an accusing brow.

She shrugged. "I was working in there when they were watching it. It was oddly compelling."

A shout went up, ripping my attention back to

the pond. Grym had disappeared again. I took two steps toward shore before Sebille grabbed my wrist, stopping me.

"He'll pull you under, Naida. You're not strong enough to help from the water."

Rustin had reached the spot where Grym had last been. He bent over the side of the boat, shouting Grym's name.

"We have to do something," I told the sprite.

She nodded, her expression pinched. Her eyes went wide and she scrunched her face again.

"What's wrong?" I asked, leaning hopefully toward the pond as Rustin tugged an oar off the boat and shoved it into the water.

"I can't..."

A large form broke the surface of the water and Grym dragged air into his lungs. I could hear him gasping all the way to shore. He was clutching the oar Rustin had dipped into the pond and Rustin was putting everything he had into trying to pull him toward the boat.

"Kick your legs," Rustin ground out, his voice breathless with effort.

Beside me, Sebille's bony frame had gone still.

"It's okay," I told her. "Look, he's got a hand on the side of the boat."

But Sebille didn't relax. "Hurry up and get back here, Rustin," she called out.

I turned to look at her as Rustin started rowing, a

dripping Grym huddled miserably in the front of the boat. "Why do you look like somebody just cut your braids?"

Sebille's fingers automatically found the fringe at the bottom of one braid and she frowned. "Did you ever watch the second episode?"

I shook my head a little too quickly. Sebille's brows lifted. It was so strange seeing the generally brightly-hued sprite with black hair and eyebrows and pasty white flesh. Well, the pasty part was kind of normal, but her freckles were gray dots across her cheeks instead of their usual warm brown color.

"You're lying."

I wasn't lying. Not really. I hadn't actually seen it all the way through, I missed the little three-second close at the end. "I caught glimpses of it as I passed through the library, that's all."

She shook her head, her light-gray gaze sliding toward the pond, filled with worry.

I turned to see how they were doing, expecting them to be near the shore. But they were still about ten yards out. Worse, they seemed to be struggling to get closer.

Grym had taken over the oars and Rustin was on his knees in the bottom of the boat, flinging water out with his cupped hands. "What's going on?" I asked the sprite.

"That boat has a leak in it."

"Why didn't you tell me?" I exclaimed, realizing

as I yelled at her that I'd known it too, on some level. That had been the niggle in my mind when I saw the boat onshore.

"I'm telling you now," Sebille yelled back. "It's not like we had a choice. Grym was going to die out there if we didn't do something."

She was right and I was being an itch with a B. "I'm sorry." I wrung my hands together. "But we need to help them."

Sebille's eyes went wide. "It's too late for that."

My head whipped around just as the boat sank below the surface, sending Grym back into the water and Rustin with him.

I gave a little shriek and ran toward the pond, my gaze locked on the frantic splashing around Grym.

Rustin's head burst from the water a beat later. Unbelievably, he was laughing. I thought he'd lost his mind.

Then he stood up.

Grym stopped flailing around and stared at Rustin for a moment before a crooked grin split his wide, handsome face. "Oh."

Rustin burst into new peals of laughter, offering the embarrassed cop a hand up.

A moment later, they pulled the boat from the water and overturned it on the shore to drain the water from the bottom.

I turned to Sebille, a sense of foreboding filling

me even before I saw that she was still frowning. "What's wrong, sprite?"

She opened her mouth to answer but didn't get the chance.

"Stop right there, thieves!"

We turned to find a scrawny, bug-eyed cop in a pale gray uniform with an extra-wide belt slung where his hips would be if only he had them.

He focused an antique-looking gun on us in two shaky hands, his hat wobbling from the quaking. "Take your paws off that there boat, ya rascals."

I couldn't help it. I grinned. "Barney Fiff, I presume?"

The man blinked in surprise, the gun wobbling in my direction. "Don't try your whiles on me, Jezebel. I caught ya red-handed. You rascals are goin' ta spend some time in the Mayberry jail."

Jumpin' Jezebels! I muttered unhappily. It was going to be really hard to find the troublesome trio from a jail cell. Unless..." Hey Deputy Fiff, you haven't by any chance seen a frog, a cat, and a hobgoblin around here, have you?"

Fiff's buggy eyes narrowed in accusation. "What is that, one of them citified jokes? A frog, a cat, and a..." His eyes narrowed to slits as he contemplated the last one. "Hobbyglobin, walk into a place of inebriation and lawlessness..."

I sighed. If the deputy thought having the

terrible threesome in Mayberry was a bad joke, he was less clueless than I'd assumed.

Next to me, Sebille snorted.

Fiff turned his glare to the sprite, and his googly eyes widened. His mouth falling open, Fiff ogled her as if he thought she was something from the fiery depths of Hades.

He could actually have been right about that.

"How about a pretty woman with a spunky pony-tail?" I asked the jittery lawman. "Have you seen her? She should be easy to spot. She's wearing a really weird skirt with a poodle on it."

Fiff twitched and jittered. "You ain't gonna distract me with your nonsense, Missy."

Dripping wet, Grym strode forward, big hands raised as the wobbly gun slid in his direction. "I'm a cop too, Deputy Fiff." He held up his hands as Fiff got noticeably more upset by his movement. "I'm just going to show you my badge." Grym slowly reached for the badge he kept in his shirt pocket and frowned. From the look on his face, I figured he'd either left the badge in his other shirt, or it had fallen out in the pond. "I seem to have lost my badge in the water…"

Got it in two.

Fiff's eyes nearly popped out of his face. "Sure ya did. I didn't fall out o' no turnip truck yesterday, Mister." The deputy whipped the gun toward the road, where the world's biggest car sat waiting in all its monochrome majesty. "Now git, you four. You have a date with a jail cell."

I grabbed my plate of pie, and we started toward the car. I don't know why the others followed the deputy's instructions. Even if he managed to fire the gun, he'd probably miss us all and somehow shoot his own foot. But I kept thinking about that blind squirrel getting the nut thing.

I was pretty sure I was just the nut to get in the way of a badly fired bullet.

———

The trip from countryside to town was ridiculously short. Television sitcom short. Lasting only about forty-five seconds. The streets looked much as I remembered them from my few times checking out the show. Sigh... Full disclosure. I watched two entire episodes before I forced myself to walk away from it. I told myself I was just spending quality time with the trio. But they'd been glassy-eyed in front of the television, totally ignoring me. The truth was that Andrew of Mayberry was oddly addictive. Even after I'd forced myself to turn away and return to my work, I'd found myself listening to the quaint dialogue from afar. I'd even left the dividing door open, so I could listen when I was in the bookstore. And I was pretty sure I'd heard Sebille whistling the theme song once or twice as she worked.

I wondered if all that was part of its magical charm. Did it reel you in with some kind of allurement spell and then hold you captive until it could suck you all the way inside?

I shuddered, drawing a questioning gaze from Sebille.

"I'm worried about Lea," I told the sprite in lieu of trying to explain my thoughts about the artifact.

I know what you're thinking, but it wasn't because I'd have to reveal my guilt in watching the show when I'd claimed I hadn't. I just didn't think the front bench seat of the enormous police car was the right place for it.

At least the wobbly deputy had finally put his gun away. Apparently, he didn't think we were going to overwhelm him as he drove us to jail.

In his world, I was sure he was probably right.

But in *my* world...

I leaned forward and peered past Sebille to the deputy. "What exactly are we going to jail for?"

He turned a theatrically shocked look on us, his lips flapping like a landed fish. "What for? You folks can't really be that clueless."

Apparently, we could. "I'm serious. We're new in town and we just want to find our friends."

"Did you or did you not take Sheriff Andrew's

personal and private property and attempt a water escape?"

I stared at him a moment, fighting to keep from impersonating my own brand of fish. "Um."

"We meant no harm. We were simply trying to rescue our friend," Rustin said from the back seat. Wayyyyyy back there. I decided I could fit four of my cute little beetle bug cars into the Mayberry-mobile.

Unfortunately, the ghost witch sounded a tad bit snotty and...well...citified. That didn't go over well with Deputy Fiff.

"Don't you backtalk me, Mister. I'm the law in these parts. And I got you under arrest."

"He wasn't backtalking, Deputy," Grym tried. "I was drowning."

Fiff frowned. "Why was you drowning?"

"Because I can't swim."

Fiff shook his head, his buggy eyes adding to the fish resemblance. "If you cain't swim, what was you doin' in that pond?" He mumbled something about dense city slickers and I fought a grin. He had us there. We couldn't exactly tell him we'd fallen into Mayberry from another world.

"I fell in," Grym said.

"Son, that water's two feet deep where you was. You expect me ta believe you was drownin' there?"

I caught Grym's gaze and gave my head a little shake. Trying to reason with Deputy Fiff was a lost cause. We'd try to speak to the Sheriff. Hopefully, he was like the Sheriff in the television show. If so, he'd not only let us out of jail, he might even help us find our friends.

I frowned at the thought, wondering where Lea had ended up and praying she was okay. I had no idea how she'd gotten separated from us. Whatever we'd done wrong, at best, had made our task in the artifact even more difficult to accomplish. And at worst...

Well, I was just hoping we'd all come out of that horrible place alive and intact.

A possibility that seemed to be getting more unlikely by the moment.

7

IN FROG FLIPPIN' MAYBERRY!

Deputy Fiff pulled up to the curb in front of the building that contained the Sheriff's Office and the Justice of the Peace. I was pretty sure they were the same thing, but there were two signs on the double doors, creating the illusion of multiple offices where there was only one.

Okay, I was splitting hairs. But it was either that or pull them right out of my head.

I was in frog flippin' Mayberry!

And so far, it was every bit as weird as I'd expected it to be.

"Now get on out of the car, and through them doors," Fiff barked in his high-pitched voice.

We piled out and filed in as barked...instructed. The space was just as I'd anticipated, with a single, large jail cell filled with homey furniture and a desk where Sheriff Andrew or his high-strung deputy could sit when they were there. The front of the building had large windows, like a storefront, that looked out on a quiet street with few cars and even fewer people. The women I saw were dressed just like I was, which made me feel a bit better.

None of the men were dressed like Grym or Rustin. However, I bit my tongue to keep from pointing it out.

Wondering how Lea was getting along with her poodle-covered skirt, I fought a smile at the same time worry niggled. I hoped she was all right.

"Just get on inside that jail cell," the deputy shrieked, swinging his oversized gun all over the place. We all ducked as we moved past him, sure he was going to let one loose in the office and clip one of us by accident.

Knowing we could just reach through the bars and grab the key on the giant ring hanging right next to the cell, we did as commanded, not overly worried.

"How long are you planning on keeping us?" Grym asked. "We have the right to post bail."

Bail? I felt my eyebrows lifting. I didn't have any Mayberry Money on me. Did Grym? I doubted it. I had no idea what kind of money they even used. Monopoly money?

Yikes! Why hadn't I thought about the money

issue? Not that there was any reference material about how to survive in a fictitious television show. If we survived the current adventure, I made a mental note to ask Archibald Pudsnecker if he knew of such a thing. And if he didn't, I'd encourage him to write it.

Yes, he was a Sorcerer of the Voids. And, no, Mayberry wasn't strictly a void. But it was close. So far, there was a definite void of common sense and brains in the place.

"You just get on inside and pipe down," Fiff barked. "Sheriff Andrew'll tell ya yore rights." The deputy grabbed the key on its giantnormous ring and locked the door, sliding the ring right back onto the hook inches away from the bars.

I grinned at Sebille and she rolled her eyes.

"Where *is* the Sheriff?" Grym asked.

Fiff flapped a hand toward the door. "The Sheriff's a busy man. He'll be around when he's ready." Then Fiff seemed to think better of answering Grym, and his skinny face darkened to ash around the cheeks. I could only guess they would be pink if we weren't living in a monochrome world. Either that or the man had a serious blood issue.

"The Sheriff's comin's and goin's ain't none o' yore concern. Now just take a seat in there and pipe down."

The outer door opened, and a well-padded

woman with upswept hair entered, carrying a tray covered with a towel. Unlike the crotchety deputy, her eyes sparkled and she had a pleasant smile on her round face. "Lunchtime, Barney."

Fiff skimmed a bug-eyed look toward us. "Now Aint Bee, you know yore supposed ta call me Deputy Fiff during work hours."

She tittered happily. "Oh Barney, don't be silly. I brought lunch for your prisoners." She gave us a wide smile. "Homemade chicken and dumplin's."

"Aint Bee makes the best chicken and dumplin's in the whole county," Fiff grumbled.

"Awe, Barney," she said, clearly pleased as she marched toward the cell.

The delicious aroma of moist fried chicken and buttery mashed potatoes wafted toward us from the contents of the tray. "That smells delicious," I said, giving the older woman a smile.

She stopped, her eyes going wide. "How did you get some of Andrew's mother's good china?"

I blinked, confused, and then followed her gaze to the plate filled with pie in my hand. The artifact I'd been instructed to bring along. "Oh, I..."

"It was sitting over there on that table," Sebille said, lying smoothly.

Aunt Bee's cheeks dimpled in a wide smile. "Oh, how careless of me. Well, you hand that on over to me. That pie's probably stale. I've got fresh pie for you here."

I had no idea how she had full chicken and dumpling meals for four people, along with dessert, on that small tray, but I didn't argue. I held it out and looked at Deputy Fiff.

He stared back for a beat before his buggy eyes achieved new levels of bugginess. "Aint Bee! You cain't go inta that cell. Them's dangerous felons right there. You wouldn't be safe."

"Pshaw!" Aunt Bee said succinctly. "You just unlock that door and let me inside, Barney Fiff. Andrew wouldn't want prisoners in his jail to starve, now would he?"

Fiff's mouth opened and closed a few times, his scrawny hands wringing his oversized deputy hat to within an inch of its life. "Sheriff Andrew wouldn't thank me for puttin' you in danger, Aint Bee. More important, I wouldn't thank myself."

The exterior door opened, and I found myself sending a plea to the goddess that it was Sheriff Andrew. Hopefully, he'd be the voice of reason in an unreasonable world.

A girl could hope, right?

Instead, it was another woman. A very familiar one. "Lea!"

My friend jerked to a stop, her pretty gaze widening as she skimmed it over us.

Barney Fiff hurried toward the door, his bent, spindly form nearly floating above the floor as he rushed over. "Thelma Lou! What are you doing here?"

I frowned. *Thelma Lou?*

Lea's slight frown smoothed as he pecked her on the cheek. "I came to bring you this." She held something up that was covered in cloth, grasping the edge of the cloth and whipping it aside.

Deputy Fiff's eyes lit up. "A slice of your chocolate, buttercream cake?" He shoved his hands onto his skinny hips and beamed at her. "Why Thelma Lou, you spoil me."

Lea, a.k.a. Thelma Lou beamed back as if she really cared what the strange little man thought. "It's nothing. I had an extra slice and thought you might like it."

Aunt Bee set the delicious-smelling tray down on the desk and hurried over to clasp Lea's hands. "What a nice surprise, dear!"

I rolled my gaze to my cellmates, finding them all staring at the little tableau beyond the bars with as much shock as I was.

"Do I smell some of your delicious chicken and dumplings?" Lea asked.

"You do. I have plenty. Would you like to stay for lunch?" Aunt Bee responded.

"Oh, I wish I could," Lea said. "I need to get home. I'm having my rose-patterned wallpaper torn down."

Aunt Bee clapped her pudgy hands. "You don't say?"

"I do! And I'm replacing it with a lovely lilac design."

I tried to catch my friend's eye. Clearly, she'd immersed herself into the whole Mayberry schtick when she found herself separated from us. I didn't blame her at all for that. What was weird was how quickly they'd accepted her into their strange universe.

Lea caught me making faces at her and blanched, rearing back. She slid a horrified glance over Sebille and clutched the pearls around her neck. Then she eyed Grym and Rustin, her attractive features softening with interest.

Unfortunately, Barney Fiff noticed. He threw a glare toward us and then hurried Lea out the door before I could think of anything to say to keep her there.

"I'll just leave you to feed the prisoners," Aunt Bee said, patting Deputy Fiff on the shoulder. "I expect Andrew will be here soon. He can smell my chicken and dumplings from clear across the county."

Fiff closed the door behind the older woman and glowered at us. "I see you tryin' ta influence the good people of Mayberry with your evil ways." Shoving his bony hands over his bony hips, he gave us his A-game glare. "You'll need ta get through *this* lawman afore you do that. And that ain't gonna happen." He tugged the oversized gun from its holster with such force he lost his grip on it and the weapon flew into the air, hilt over barrel, smacking into the bars of the cell and clattering toward the floor.

We all yelped and took cover behind the homey furniture.

Fiff scurried over and retrieved the gun, shoving it into its holster with another flush of gray cheeks. He looked slightly sheepish. Opening the cell door, Fiff shoved the tray at Grym and then quickly closed and locked it again. He headed for the exterior door. "I'm off to lunch now. No funny business while I'm gone."

And then he just left.

Silence pulsed between us for a beat. For my part, I was too shocked at...well...everything, to speak.

My friends must have been suffering a similar emotion. Finally, Sebille muttered, "Holy dancing dumplings. What just happened here?"

"I hate to say it," Rustin responded. "But it appears that Lea's been pulled in too deep."

We all looked at him. Sebille was frowning. Grym looked...well...grim.

My stomach tightened painfully, even as my mind tried to deny what he'd said. "What does that mean, exactly?" I asked.

Rustin looked devastated. "She's become one of them."

My knees gave out, and I all but fell into the rocking chair behind me. Thank goodness for the comfortable, flowered chintz cushions in the chair, or it might have hurt. "We need to get out of here. Lea needs us as much as Hobs, Slimy, and Wicked do."

Rustin skimmed a worried gaze in my direction. "I don't think you understand, Naida. We can't help Lea. She's part of the artifact now. She's gone."

I shook my head and kept shaking it even after he'd finished speaking because I was terrified that, if I stopped denying it, his assertion that Lea was lost would be true. "I won't accept that."

Rustin just stared at the floor. Grym gave me a sad look, which made me mad. So I looked at the sprite, daring her with my gaze to give up on Lea so easily.

I was happy to see that Sebille was in my corner. She looked mad too.

Really mad.

Stomping over to the bars, she reached through and tugged the giant ring off the wall, quickly unlocking the cell.

"What are you doing?" Grym asked.

She glowered in his direction. "You can sit here and follow crazy people rules, or you can come with us. I don't give a frog's flipper what you do. I'm going after our friends."

Grym opened his mouth and closed it, expelling a frustrated breath.

I looked at Rustin and he nodded. "We're not accomplishing anything here."

"They'll just find you again and put you back in here," Grym argued. He crossed his muscular arms over his chest, staring angrily at me.

I snorted. "You think Fiff is going to find us?"

"Not the idiot deputy, no," Rustin said. "But you forget he's part of the artifact. His persona is just window dressing. The artifact is running this show, and it's not stupid. It's deadly and determined."

Sebille opened the door and stepped through, throwing the two men a look that dared them to stay. "We knew that when we came inside, ghost witch," she said. "I'm not going to curl up into the fetal position now and give up. Are you?"

He looked like he was thinking about it.

"Look, Sebille, Naida," Grym spoke in placating tones. "We're not giving up. We're just trying to take the path of least resistance. Sheriff Andrew is the reasonable one. We just need to talk to him, and he'll let us go. Then we won't have to look over our shoulders the whole time we're here."

"*If* he shows up," I argued. "And *if* he lets us go. Like Rustin said, there's no guarantee they're the same in here as they are on the television show.

Andrew might be a jerk. A blood-thirsty killer. We have no way of knowing."

"Fiff seems pretty harmless," Grym said.

Rustin sighed. "He does, but they're right. Like I said, the artifact is running things, not the characters from the show." He nodded at me. "I'm in. But we'll need to move fast. In TV time, Fiff should be returning any minute from his lunch."

8

IT WEREN'TNOTHIN', SUGAR

G rym did a quick search of the desk, just in case Fiff or Andrew documented the arrival of the cat, the frog, Hobs, or Lea. He didn't find anything, but we didn't give him much time to look.

I grabbed the never-ending pie artifact, which had mysteriously returned to the cell after Aunt Bee left. I had no idea what good it was going to do me, but I trusted Adolfo's advice to bring it and figured it must have a purpose.

Sebille was watching the street so we'd have warning when Fiff came back. As Grym closed the last desk drawer, she turned back to us. "He's coming."

We ran to the door and looked out as Fiff stopped an old woman with a cane who'd waddled across the middle of the street. He seemed to be yelling at her for jaywalking and she was looking befuddled by his waving arms and bugged-out eyes. When Fiff dug into his pocket and came up with a pair of handcuffs, that was our cue to go.

"It's going to be really crowded in that cell if we don't get out of here," Grym said.

I nodded. "Let's head left as soon as we hit the sidewalk and enter the alleyway between this building and the next."

"Walk slowly until we turn the corner," Grym advised. "Nothing catches a cop's attention faster than people running away from him."

Grym led the way out the door and we fell in behind him. It was good that he was in front because I'd have run, despite what he said. I was sure I could feel Fiff's bulgy gaze between my shoulder blades, and I ran up on Grym's heels a few times trying to get away from it.

We managed to reach the alley before the deputy started shrieking at us. As we turned the corner I was relieved to start running. We ran for a few minutes, finding the monochromatic town a maze with few clues about where we were at any given moment.

We finally stopped running when we reached a small park with a cute little white lattice gazebo at its center. We collapsed onto the benches of a gray wood picnic table, panting.

After a moment, Sebille asked. "Where do we start?"

"Hex," I said, without hesitation.

They all looked at me.

"We need to find Hex," I explained. "If the cat hasn't been co-opted by the artifact, she's our best hope of waking Lea up."

Though Rustin didn't look convinced, he nodded. "Why don't you and Grym look for Hex and Sebille and I will see if we can find Hobs, Mr. Slimy, and Mr. Wicked."

"I'm actually hoping Hex will still be herself and she can find Mr. Wicked for us," I told him.

Sebille started walking along the path surrounding the park.

Rustin nodded. "Meet back here in an hour?"

We all agreed and went our separate ways. The last I saw of the sprite and the ghost witch, they were heading toward the edge of town. I could see the pond where we'd landed in the near distance and realized it would have been the logical spot to look for Slimy. The little green guy always seemed to find his way to a pond, wherever he was.

"Horned hippopotamus hats," I grumbled under my breath. If Fiff hadn't come along and pulled us in, we might have found the frog immediately.

I sighed.

"What's wrong?" Grym asked.

I shook my head.

"Any idea where we'll find Hex?" he asked, his gaze skimming the area around us.

I pointed to a street of tidy houses just outside of town. "That looks like as good a place as any to start. Unless she got separated from Hex, which seems unlikely since she was holding her when she landed, we should find them together."

Grym nodded. "Let's hope those people don't mind a couple of strangers skulking around." He gave me a crooked grin. "Maybe we should act like we're a couple, just strolling down the street."

I knew he was right, but I couldn't help narrowing my eyes suspiciously. "A couple, huh?"

He shrugged. "It's just a suggestion."

And if I was being honest with myself, it was a good one. "Okay. We don't want the neighbors to call Fiff."

"No, we do not," Grym agreed, with feeling.

When we reached the street, I slipped my arm through his and we strolled along the sidewalk, heads on a swivel. I tried to ignore the firm warmth of his big body pressed against my side. It felt good. And that made me kind of mad. And that was stupid. I'd mostly forgiven Grym for what I'd perceived as his disloyalty for turning me into the Société of Dire Magic. On a rational level, I understood he'd just been doing his job. On an emotional level, my feelings were hurt.

But he did feel warm and safe, if still a little damp, pressed against me.

And I couldn't deny to myself that I liked that closeness.

"Hello!"

We turned to find a middle-aged woman with a damp sheet in her hands. She was standing in front of a laundry line, a basket at her feet. She smiled at us, her lips dark and smooth with layers of lipstick and her hair perfectly done up in a little flip. She wore a cotton dress, not unlike the one I was wearing, and dainty little shoes that had straps around the ankles.

Thinking of how I usually looked when I did my laundry, I fought back a grin. The "real" life portrayed in the shows from the 1960s was nothing like reality. Or, at least I hoped it wasn't. I hated to think of all those women getting dressed up every morning to clean the toilets.

I was lucky if I was wearing more than just my underwear when I cleaned *my* house.

"Hi!" I said, pasting a grin on my face and giving her a little wave.

"You must be new in town," the woman said, clipping the pristine white sheet to the line and bending to pick up the empty basket. She swayed toward us. "It's always nice to have new blood in Maybury."

She scanned a pair of light-colored eyes appreciatively over Grym and something ugly bloomed in my chest. Something that felt too much like jealousy for my comfort. I pressed more tightly against his side and offered the woman my hand. "Naida Griffith. It's nice to meet you."

The woman clasped my fingers in a limp grip. "Polly Smith." She turned to Grym, offering him her hand and gripping his as if he were a lifeline in the middle of the ocean. "It's such a pleasure."

Grym smiled widely, holding her hand a beat longer than strictly necessary. "It's nice to meet you, Polly. My name's Grym. We *are* new in town, and we're looking for just the right neighborhood. We ran into a nice lady downtown who said this was the best place to live in town."

"Oh?" Polly asked, arching a brow that appeared to be nothing but pencil. "Who might that be?"

Grym looked at me, frowning as if trying to remember. "Thelma Lou?"

I nodded.

He shook his head. "I'm afraid I can't remember her last name."

Polly's overpainted upper lip curled. "Thelma lives down there. Third house from the end of the street. She's new too."

I felt my eyebrows climb higher on my forehead. If the artifact recognized Lea as new, maybe there was still hope?

Grym nodded, giving me a bright smile. "See, honey, I told you this was the right street."

Her lips compressing, Polly glowered at me. "What do you all want with Thelma Lou?"

I held her gaze, an easy lie not popping into my mind.

Grym saved me. "She promised us a tour of the neighborhood."

Polly's glower transformed into a leer. She sidled over and draped herself over one of Grym's broad shoulders. "Is that all? Why, sugar, you don't need Thelma for that. I can give you that tour."

"Thanks for the offer, but..."

"We'd really appreciate that," Grym said, cutting off my rejection. "Do you know everybody on the street?" He dropped my arm like a hot potato and let the "hot to trot" Polly tug him down the street. "Most everybody," she said. "That there's Old Man Aberdeen's place. He don't like people steppin' on his lawn." She rolled her eyes, making me feel as if I was spending time with the sprite. "But the man does grow prize winnin' roses, I'll give him that."

I scanned the front of the clapboard home, a pale color that could be anything from tan to light green for all I knew. There were indeed roses all across the front of the home and filling the front corners in carefully tended raised beds. There might not have been any color to showcase the full splendor of the flowers, but the air was rich with the scent of them.

Grym nodded toward a small play area at the center of the street. "That's a pretty little park."

Polly's gaze barely left the detective's strong jaw long enough to acknowledge the space. But she did grimace slightly. "Yes. Unfortunately, it draws the little monsters like bees to honey."

"Little monsters?" I asked, nursing a weird hope that she was talking about Hobs.

"Children." Polly shuddered. "I can't stand the little hooligans myself." She fixed a feral smile on Grym. "I consider myself lucky I didn't conceive before Mr. Smith passed."

She winked at Grym, her message sent. She was a widow. And she apparently thought Grym would be interested in knowing that.

Watching him touching her arm as she fawned all over him, I frowned. I could see why she'd think that.

We approached Lea's, aka Thelma Lou's home and I saw a familiar small gray form draped over the windowsill inside the house. "Oh, she has a cat!" I exclaimed happily. My strange glee earned me a double-barreled eyebrow arching from the amorous Polly. "Yes. Nasty critters. And they get into everything." She shook her head.

"Get into everything?" Grym asked.

"Yes. She lets it run around the neighborhood and the nasty creature is always getting into people's business. Yesterday, it walked across Old Man Aberdeen's yard and squatted in his rose bed. I thought he was going to drop dead of apoplexy on the spot."

"I'm sure it didn't hurt anything," I said, frowning. The woman didn't like anyone or anything, apparently.

Polly shrugged. "Lately, it's been up to even more trouble than usual. It ran in front of Pearla Rogers this morning and almost sent her to her knees. She was carrying bags of food from the diner downtown and didn't see the thing until it was too late."

"We should go talk to Thelma Lou," I told Grym.

He nodded. "Thank you for giving us the tour," Grym told Polly, trying to extricate himself from her octopus-like grip.

"It was nothin', sugar." She winked again. "I'd be happy ta do it anytime."

He finally got free of her with a less-than-gentle tug that sent her stumbling away but still smiling, and we started up the sidewalk to Lea's house.

Hex watched our approach but didn't react except to blink slowly at us.

Not a good sign.

I rang the bell. There was no answer.

"Maybe she's out back," Grym suggested.

I nodded and we hurried around the house to a small, neatly-kept back yard surrounded by a low picket fence. There was a tidy flagstone patio, accessed by a small door that stood ajar. On the patio was a wrought-iron table with two iron chairs. I didn't see Lea, but there was a glass of iced tea on the table, sweat running down the tall glass and dripping through the ornate metal to the flagstones beneath the table.

"It looks like she was just here," Grym said.

Stepping over the short fence, we headed for the door into the house.

Grym pushed it open, one hand reaching for a weapon he didn't have, and called out, "Miss Thelma?"

Silence met his call, so he pushed the door wider and stepped inside. "Miss Thelma, are you okay?"

At first, I thought she'd left the house. But then I heard a soft noise that sounded like someone in pain. My gaze met Grym's, and he plunged all the way through the door.

We found her lying on the floor in front of an ancient refrigerator, her hair spread across the well-worn wood in a glossy pool.

I hurried over. "Lea! Are you all right? What happened?"

She sat up with Grym's help, her eyes finding mine even as she reached for her head and groaned. "I must have fallen and hit my head."

She frowned, rubbing her temples. "What did you call me?"

I realized my mistake and forced an innocent look onto my face. "Thelma Lou? Why?" I felt bad lying to my best friend, but she was already hurting, and I didn't want to give her even more stress. Telling her she was an Earth witch from decades in the future seemed more than likely to do that.

"Let me help you up off this floor." Grym grabbed her under the arms and helped her stand. Lea swayed, her face turning grayer as she stood. "I should probably sit down."

We helped her into a vinyl-covered chair at a round wooden table.

"I don't know what's wrong with me," she said, sighing. "I must be coming down with something."

Lea seemed to remember she didn't know us very well. Certainly not well enough to find us in her kitchen. She frowned at Grym and then me. "I've met you before, haven't I?"

I nodded. "At the jail."

Her eyes went wide with horror. "Oh!"

Grym lifted his hands. "Nothing to worry about, Miss Thelma. We're not here to hurt anybody. We just wanted to ask you a couple of questions."

I found a glass in the cupboards and filled it with water from the faucet, handing it to her. "Here, drink this."

She drank, much too docile for my taste. If she was herself, my friend would have been demanding answers at that point.

"Meow!" A soft, warm body wound through my legs and jumped up into Lea's lap. She bent down and kissed the little cat between her soft ears. "Hello, sweet girl. I'm all right."

Hex glared at me as if Lea's condition was my fault. I bit back the urge to defend myself. "What a pretty cat," I said instead. "What's her name?"

Lea blinked rapidly as if trying to remember. "I... I'm not sure." She sagged in the chair. "Something's very wrong with me."

"How long have you been feeling bad?" Grym asked.

Lea shrugged. "A couple of days now." She sighed, running her hand over the cat's soft gray fur. "Hex has been worried about me."

"Hex?" I asked, my gaze flying to Grym's.

"Yes, um, I guess that's her name." She seemed to consider it, and the thought process didn't make her look happy. "Such a strange name for a cat."

Not if you were an earth witch, I thought to myself. "It's a perfect name," I said aloud, giving my friend a reassuring smile. "She's adorable." A thought occurred to me, and I gave it voice before I had a chance to reconsider. "You haven't seen another cat like her around here, have you?"

Lea frowned, rubbing her temple. "No. Why do you ask?"

Hex's dark gaze rose to mine and she cocked her head, her tail doing a slow slide across the floor behind her.

Something in her gaze gave me pause. There was

an intelligence there that made me wonder if she'd understood my question. Being Mr. Wicked's litter-mate, it would make perfect sense if she had. He not only seemed to understand what I said to him, he often seemed to be a few steps ahead of me in the thought process.

So I stared at Hex a moment longer, feeling as if the little cat was trying to tell me something.

The moment was broken by Grym's deep voice. "Naida?"

I blinked and realized I'd gotten totally distracted. Glancing his way, I had the sense I'd missed something important. "I'm sorry. I was wool-gathering."

"Thelma Lou said that Hex has been acting strangely. That she keeps trying to get into Old Man Aberdeen's house. Apparently, Thelma spent an hour looking for her yesterday and found her perched on an exterior windowsill of his home." He lifted his brows, trying to beam an unspoken message into my brain that I couldn't decipher.

Whatever happened to the old-fashioned method of communication called *speaking*? I was just as much a modern girl as the next guy. But, *holy window willies*, some things should never go out of style.

In exasperation, I widened my eyes at him, and he sighed.

"Maybe Wicked's in the house," Grym finally said.

"Who's Wicked? What are you talking about?" Lea asked, sounding a bit panicked.

Ah, okay. Maybe unspoken communication had been a good idea. It simplified things.

Who knew?

I looked at her. "A friend of mine lost her cat, and he looks a lot like Hex. We were hoping to help her find him."

Lea reached out and snatched up her cat, snuggling her close. "Hex is mine. Your friend should look somewhere else for her cat."

"We weren't…"

"You should go now," Lea said, her face mottled with splotches as fear and anger turned her unreasonable.

"We really weren't…" I tried again.

Lea stood, clutching Hex as if the Hounds of Hades were trying to get her, and pointed a rigid finger toward the door. "Go!"

9

I HAVE ME SOME ABORIGINALS TO SUBDUE!

"That went well," I told Grym.

"At least we have an idea of where to start looking for Wicked."

I nodded. "Did you get the impression Hex was Hex?"

"It scares me that I know what you just said. But, yeah. At least on some level. She's still herself. But Lea's struggling. I wonder if her mind is trying to kick off the effects of the artifact?"

"That would be good, right?" I asked.

Grim shrugged. "I just don't know."

We hit the sidewalk, heading back down the street toward the home with the prize-winning roses. If Old Mr. Aberdeen was the type to yell at kids for stepping on his grass, how would he take two strangers showing up at his door uninvited, looking for a cat?

Probably not well.

Nobody answered Mr. Aberdeen's door. We discussed it and finally decided to try the back door, though it would probably send the old man into orbit as a level five intrusion.

The back yard of the house was just grass. No trees. No roses. No patio.

In fact, we realized as we rounded the corner of the home, there wasn't even a door on the back.

Or windows.

"What in the..." Grym said.

It hit me immediately what was going on because I'd seen it recently. In the abyss. "The back isn't formed yet," I murmured to myself.

"What?" Grym asked, looking perplexed.

"I saw this in the abyss. Only the parts that are needed are created. Old Mr. Aberdeen's persona apparently doesn't need a back yard."

"Or, like you said, it just hasn't formed yet."

I realized what he was saying. "Like Mr. Aberdeen is new to the artifact?"

Grym nodded.

"You don't think..."

A crash sounded inside the house, followed by a shrill scream. Grym and I took off running and barely slowed as we hit the small front porch. Grym pounded hard on the door, calling the man's name.

I tried to peer in through the large front window,

but the drapes were closed and I couldn't see anything through the small center crack.

Grym reared back and punched a kick into the door. The sound of splintering wood filled the following silence.

I looked anxiously up and down the street. Luckily, no one else seemed interested in the sound of someone breaking into Old Mr. Aberdeen's place. There wasn't so much as a twitching curtain.

"Mr. Aberdeen!" Grym called again. He waited a second longer and then kicked the door again. Nothing.

"Maybe you should make like a gargoyle," I told him.

He glanced up and down the street and apparently saw what I'd seen. Nobody was watching. A strange look came over his face, like he was straining. Then he looked down at his hands, frowning.

"What's wrong?" I asked.

"My magic isn't working."

That was bad. "Should we try kicking the door again?"

Grym kicked the door three more times before it finally crashed inward. For something that was basically made up from the ether, that Mayberry house sure was sturdy.

The door flew open and crashed against the wall with a horrendous crunching sound. Grym dove through the door with me hot on his heels.

A man flew toward us, wild gray hair flying and a heavy frying pan clutched in his gnarled hands. His eyes were wild, his mouth open in another feral scream, and he was wearing only boxer shorts and a stained wife-beater tee shirt.

"Mongrels!" he shrieked and I yelped, diving sideways as the pan sliced through the air where my head had been.

Grym jumped in the opposite direction, hitting the couch with his knees and falling into it.

The flowered divan slammed into the wall as the elderly man spun, more agile than a gentleman of his age should have been, and headed toward Grym with the pan.

The detective held up his blocky hands. "Sir! Mr. Aberdeen, we're here to help."

Long, stringy arms that were covered in an abundance of silvery hair swung the pan downward, barely missing Grym and smacking the sofa seat.

Grym slapped his hand down on top of the potentially deadly weapon so the elderly man couldn't heft it back up.

"Let it go, sonny!" Mr. Aberdeen yelled. "I have me some Aboriginals to subdue!"

I caught Grym's eye and lifted my brows. His lips quivered in a smile. "No aboriginals here, sir. We heard a scream and wondered if you were all right."

A high-pitched squeal sounded from the next room. I turned my head in time to see a chandelier swing past the arched doorway, a small, white projectile flying from it with arms outstretched and enormous eyes bulging with excitement.

The small projectile hit the chair across the room and it went down under his weight. He landed face down, arms and legs akimbo, with an audible "umph!".

My heart rate spiked and I shoved to my feet. "Grym!"

But he wasn't paying attention. He'd nearly managed to get the old man's fingers unclenched from around the pan and was still trying to reason with him. "Sir, I'm going to need you to not hit me with this pan."

"Grym, I yelled again. Look!"

Just then, the downed projectile lifted his oversized head, pointed ears twitching with delight, and yelled, "Again!"

Grym forgot about the pan and Mr. Aberdeen and looked across the room just as Hobs spotted me and shoved to his feet, running into my arms with a delighted cackle.

"Miss, you came!"

"Of course I came. I couldn't leave you in this place. I'd miss you too much." I tapped the end of his nose. "Besides, Sebille is devastated without you." I kissed him on a plump, soft cheek and pulled him in for a hug, enjoying his familiar frosted brownie scent.

"I thought I'd never see you again, Miss," he said, nestling his head against my shoulder.

Tears burned my eyes. I took a shuddering breath and...

Clangggggggg!

Turned just in time to see Grym folding toward the couch cushions from the application of a frying pan to the temple.

"Again!" shrieked the hobgoblin joyfully, earning a repressive glower from me.

Grym held the towel against his head, occasionally adjusting it to place the ice cubes that were wrapped in the thin cloth in a more strategic spot on the giant goose egg he sported there.

"Sorry about that, sonny," said the old man. "Me and the kid was just playin' a game. I mighta gotten a bit worked up."

The *kid* in question chuckled happily and stuffed a chunk of pie into his mouth, his cheeks covered in more filling than the slice he was finishing off. I was glad I'd brought the never-ending slice of pie plate with me. Hobs was characteristically hungry.

"The kid was havin' fun," Aberdeen said, shrugging. "I figured there weren't no harm."

"Hobs might not be the best barometer for that,"

I told Aberdeen. "He's into self-sabotage in a big way."

"Self what now?"

"He thinks it's fun to pretend he's Wile E. Coyote," Grym said, fixing the hobgoblin with a less-than-friendly look. "And apparently he thinks its fun to watch me take a frying pan to the head too."

Hobs grabbed another chunk of pie from the pretty china plate and grinned, totally without remorse.

"I don't know nothin' about that," Aberdeen said. He fixed an affectionate look on Hobs. "But he sure is a fun little guy."

Remembering the crotchety old man Polly the oversexed neighbor had described, I had trouble picturing Aberdeen joining in Hobs' questionable games. But I'd seen it with my own eyes, hadn't I?

I forked up a bite of the pie in front of me and chewed it slowly, thinking about how best to broach the subject of our visit. While I was beyond relieved to find Hobs, we were still missing two friends.

Grym beat me to it. "Your neighbor said she'd seen a cat that looked like hers at your house. Do you, by any chance, have a gray cat with dark eyes?"

Okay, not exactly what Lea had said, but close enough, and it should get us where we needed to go.

"Nope."

Or not.

"But the kid has one."

As the meaning of his words sank deep, something that had wrung tight and ugly through my belly slowly untangled. I suddenly found it easier to take a deep breath. I looked at Hobs. "Wicked's here with you?"

"Yes, Miss. He's looking."

I frowned. "Looking? For what? For Slimy?"

"Who's Slimy?" Aberdeen asked, plucking pie from the scraggly beard covering his chin.

"Um...another...kid," I finally said.

"That's an odd name for a kid," Aberdeen said, looking disgusted.

"He's an odd kid," Grym said, his lips twitching.

Aberdeen shrugged.

I watched him for a moment, something about the man bothering me.

"Do you know where Slimy is, Hobs?" Grym asked.

"Swimming," Hobs said, throwing a strange glance at Aberdeen. Though it would be totally out of character for Hobs to show restraint over any situation, I couldn't help feeling as if he was trying not to say too much in front of the elderly man.

The room around us darkened suddenly. I turned to look out the large window overlooking the front yard and spotted the cause. The sky had gone from the pale gray of what would probably be blue if we weren't in a black and white world, to a charcoal gray that was almost black.

"What's happening?" Grym asked as Aberdeen visibly tensed.

The old man surged to his feet. "Dagnabbit!" He hurried out of the room and disappeared down the hallway.

Hobs jumped up. "It's coming," the hobgoblin said as he grabbed another slice of pie and shot toward the front door, his form a pale blur on the air.

Grym and I were right behind him. By the time we hit the sidewalk at the front of the house, the entire neighborhood was filled with people, every small porch holding two to four people, men and women, young and old.

But nobody spoke. Everyone just stood on their stoops and stared up at the darkening sky.

Grym and I moved out into the yard so we could see better. I realized there was no scent of ozone in the air. No moisture. No thunder or lightning in the distance.

The sky above wasn't filled with storm clouds and there was no wind to herald a coming storm. The air was almost too still.

"This isn't a storm," Grym said, his handsome face dark with worry.

"Where did Hobs go?" I asked, glancing around.

"No idea."

I turned to find Polly a couple of houses down, standing in the yard like we were and staring toward the sky. "Polly! Did you see a little guy with a piece of pie run through here?"

She didn't move. Didn't turn her head. It was as if she didn't even hear me speak, though I was sure I'd shouted the question plenty loud enough. I scanned another look at the other people on the street. None of them had moved.

They all appeared mesmerized by whatever was boiling above our heads.

Except for one little boy, who stood a few feet away from the family directly across the street. He was staring at us instead of the sky, his tiny hands shoved into his pockets and a messy fringe of hair falling into his eyes.

Grym's voice pulled my attention back to the sky. "Something's happening," he said.

He was right. A circular spot had formed at the center of the darkness. It was enormous, encircling most of the street where we stood, and abyss-level black.

The eerie black circle was spinning, like a vortex, the occasional lighter wisp threading through it highlighting the speed at which it spun. The horizon began to twist, the upper corners folding inward and the center rippling, as it seemed to be sucked up into the spinning sky.

The ground beneath my feet jerked suddenly, sending me to the ground as if a rug had been yanked out from under me.

Grym managed to keep his feet but barely. He crouched beside me to widen his base of support.

"What in the world is going on?" I asked, my hands clenching the grass beneath them.

"I don't know, Naida. But whatever it is, I don't like the look of it."

"Do you think it knows we're here?"

The horizon was still narrowing. The distant ground lifted toward the sky, rising into the vortex as if the maelstrom were a giant vacuum cleaner sucking it up. Around us, the homes started to creak and groan as the ground beneath them shifted.

Terror clawed its way down my spine and sent my blood roaring through my ears. "Grym!" I shoved upright, ready to run but having no idea where I could go. We were in the grip of a power so much stronger than any of us. An evil force unlike anything we'd ever faced.

And I felt helpless against it.

Aberdeen's door slammed open and he flew out of the house, a double-barreled shotgun clutched in his bony hands. He was still wearing only his underclothes and his longish gray hair flew around his head with abandon as he jerked to a stop in the middle of the yard and aimed the gun toward the sky. "You're not gonna take me alive, ya rottin' varmint!" he screamed, and then he racked the big gun and let 'er rip toward the boiling sky.

Boom!

The sound hit my ears like a fist and I covered them, ducking my head as if he were shooting at me.

Rack...Boom!

It slammed into my brain, making my head feel like 100 tiny soldiers wearing golf cleats were dancing over it.

Rack...Boom!

Something shifted in the center of the vortex. I grabbed Grym's arm, intending to warn him that something was changing, and the center blinked open.

A jolt of lightning speared from the center and shot downward, heading right for Mr. Aberdeen.

Grym's muscled arm tore from my grasp and he threw himself sideways, smacking into the old man just as the shotgun went off again.

"No!" I screamed.

The thick beam of sizzling electricity slammed into the ground where Aberdeen had been, ripping an eight-inch-wide hole in the grass that sent dirt and grass spraying.

A heavy clump of dirt hit me in the face, slamming into my nose in a painful blow. I went down under the attack and hit my head hard on the ground.

Dazed and bleeding from the strike, I rolled over with a groan. Distant echoes thumped against my benumbed eardrums and I shoved upright, scraping the back of my hand under my nose and finding blood.

Then I remembered why I needed to get off the ground. *Grym!*

My terrified gaze swung to the spot where he'd been, finding a still smoking hole in the earth. And just beyond that hole were two bodies, both covered in dirt and grass and something that might have been blood. It was hard to tell in a monochrome world.

But there was one thing I could tell for sure, and it nearly made my heart stop beating.

Neither of them was moving. Not even a little bit.

10

FESTERING FROG FARTS!

"Grym!"

Across the street, a door closed with a firm thump. Then another and another. I glanced around me and saw that everyone had gone back inside their homes.

There had been exactly zero reaction to the world-eating vortex in the sky.

Not even a shrug.

I hurried over and dropped to my knees beside the detective. "Grym?" I grabbed his shoulder, giving him a gentle but insistent nudge. "Are you okay?"

He didn't move at first, making my stomach clench, but then he groaned softly and rolled over, exposing a dazed-looking Aberdeen beneath him.

The older man looked a little wild-eyed, but I was happy to see he'd lost his shotgun when Grym barreled into him. "Is it dead?" Aberdeen asked, blinking at me.

I wondered at the man's thought process. That he believed a shotgun could have any effect at all on a massive vortex in the sky was clearly alarming. "What was that thing?" I asked him.

He flopped around like a landed fish for a beat, and I realized he was trying to get off the ground. Grym and I each took an arm and helped him up.

On his feet again, Aberdeen glared up at the sky. "That's the thing that took me."

Grym and I shared a look.

"Took you?" Grym asked, watching the other man carefully.

Aberdeen nodded. "Every day I lose a bit more of my life." He looked sad, his faded gaze sliding toward the sky again. With the vortex gone, it looked peaceful, filled with fluffy white clouds as if the world hadn't almost ended moments earlier. "I don't remember many details anymore."

"But you remember something," I told him, grabbing his hand. "We're here to stop it."

He nodded. "That's what the kid said."

"His name's Hobs," I said, giving the man a smile. "He and Mr. Wicked and Mr. Slimy were taken by the thing too. We came to get them back."

Aberdeen stared at me, his mouth working as if he wasn't sure what to say.

"Mr. Aberdeen, have you met the young woman down the street? Thelma Lou?"

Aberdeen scraped a large hand over his jaw, the raspy sound of overlong whiskers filling the air. "Pretty little thing." He frowned. "She's new too."

"Yes!" I said, getting excited. "She's our friend. We got separated when we came here and she doesn't remember who she is."

Aberdeen sighed. "It pulls your memories away and puts others in their place." The old man shook his head. "Nasty business."

"Yes. Do you have any idea how we can help her remember?"

Aberdeen gave a firm shake of his head. "No hope there, hon. If she don't remember there's no hope."

Festering frog farts!

"Did you always remember?" Grym asked.

"Did I? I guess so. I must have."

Grym looked at me, and I saw the point he'd been trying to make. That it was possible Aberdeen had gone through the same process Lea seemed to be going through.

I tried to grasp onto that possibility. Lea was confused. She was struggling. Maybe her memories were trying to come back to her.

A warm breeze slid past and Hobs was suddenly there. "Miss, can you come? I need to show something."

I nodded. "Thanks, Mr. Aberdeen. We'll let you know if we find a way out of here."

He didn't seem to hear me. He'd turned and was heading toward his home, his steps heavy. He looked so weary. So sad. And I wondered how long he'd been the only one in Mayberry who knew what was going on.

"Lead the way, Hobs," Grym said.

"Hellooo!"

We turned to find Lea, aka Thelma Lou hurrying toward us, Hex trotting along at her feet. She had one of the clips I'd used to hold my hair off my face in her hand. "You left this at my house."

"Oh." I reached out and took it. "Thanks. How are you feeling?"

"I'm just peachy," she said, a television smile stretched across her face. I noticed the poodle skirt was looking a bit dingy. Apparently, the Mayberry artifact didn't return things to new once they'd been soiled or damaged.

That probably explained why Aberdeen looked so disheveled.

"That's good."

She frowned at the plate in my hand. "Do you always carry a slice of pie around with you?"

I stared at the pie on the plate. Apple. I knew from experience that the type of pie changed. Once the piece on the plate was eaten, a different slice of pie appeared to replace it. I had a sudden thought. There had to have been a reason I'd brought the stupid thing with me. I held it back out to Lea. "Actually, I brought this for you."

Lea started to reach for it and then stopped, her cheeks darkening. "Oh. Thank you kindly. But I don't eat sweets."

I thought of the cake she'd brought to Fiff earlier. I realized I hadn't seen the rest of the cake in her kitchen, though she'd implied she'd baked it. Had the artifact put it in her hands and nudged her toward the jail? And, if so, why?

Try as I might, I couldn't talk Lea into trying the pie. I looked at Grym. He was staring after Aberdeen, looking thoughtful. He suddenly grabbed the plate. "I have an idea." Hurrying after the elderly man, Grym spoke a few words with Aberdeen and handed him the plate.

I was pleased to see that the old man's step was a bit lighter the rest of the way into the house.

Grym rejoined us. "You ready to go see what Hobs found?"

I nodded. Looking at Lea's pleasant but clueless expression, I blinked back tears. On impulse, I gave her a hug. "Take care of yourself. If you don't mind, I'd like to come back to visit?"

"That would be lovely," my best friend responded with perfect plastic-coated manners.

I forced myself to turn away from her, my heart

breaking. The only way I could help Lea was to find a way to kill the artifact.

"What did you find, Hobs?" Grym asked as we hurried to keep up with the hobgoblin.

"A place, Mr. Grym. A scary place."

My steps faltered and I sucked back. "A scary place? Why is there a scary place in Mayberry? And why would we go there?" I asked.

Hobs chuckled as if I were joking. Which I was decidedly not.

He led us past the small empty playground, whose swings were swaying under a phantom influence that gave me chills. In the distance, on a raised road that wound away from town and into the countryside, the Sheriff's car drove slowly past. The enormous, boxy vehicle was being driven by a dark-haired man who had a stern face topped by dark eyebrows that slashed over a hostile gaze.

Sheriff Andrew didn't look nearly as friendly as he had on television.

I shuddered, wishing I could hide from the assessing gaze he scraped over us as he drove on past.

In the distance, the little pond we'd pulled Grym out of when we'd arrived sparkled prettily, even its inherent grayness not taking away from the picturesque little spot. "Are you taking us to the pond?" I asked.

"No, Miss."

Hobs was moving fast but not nearly as fast as he could have, and he seemed focused on something other than us at the moment, unwilling to chat.

I suddenly wondered how Sebille and Rustin were doing. "Have you seen Sebille?" I asked Hobs.

"Yes, Miss. She's at the scary place."

"Rustin too?"

Hobs nodded, skipping across the dusty grass.

Looming up ahead of us, was one of those giant concrete tunnels, or culverts, I thought they were called, cut beneath the road to provide drainage if the pond beyond the road flooded. I guessed, from the slashes of street art coating its surface, that the tunnel provided more than that. "I can't believe they have graffiti here," I told Grym, laughing.

But he was frowning. "That's not graffiti, Naida," Grym said.

"It's a working," a voice said from a nearby copse of trees.

I jumped, clapping a hand over my heart, as Sebille and Rustin stepped out of the trees. "You scared me half to death."

"Sorry," Rustin said, looking sheepish. "We were hiding from the Sheriff. He's looking for us."

I thought of the beefy old car rolling slowly down the road and the dark face of the Sheriff behind the wheel. "Did you do something?"

Rustin and Sebille shared a look.

"What?" Grym asked.

Rustin stared at Sebille, willing her to respond. She finally sighed. "I might have accidentally brought this with me." She pulled her cell phone out of an oversized pocket of her dress.

I felt my eyes go wide. "Oh no, Sebille! Your mother told us that would be really bad."

She rolled her eyes. "I didn't do it on purpose."

Grym and I glared at her.

"There's no sense beating her about the head and shoulders now," Rustin said. "Believe me, I've already yelled at her. The Sheriff seems to be tuned into that phone somehow. He's like a bloodhound with the thing."

"That's why we came down here," Sebille said. "We were going to throw it into the pond. Then we ran into Hobs and the cat."

My eyes went wide. "Wicked's here?"

Hobs nodded enthusiastically. "He's by the pond."

"And Slimy?" I asked, hopeful.

"We left him there when we came. He didn't like it near the buildings. He said there weren't enough flies."

My chest loosened as some of my worry slid away. "That's good."

"You said these symbols are a working?" Grym asked Rustin. "Any chance they're the engine behind this artifact?"

"Wouldn't that be sweet?" I asked rhetorically. I

followed him over to the concrete tunnel, where rows and rows of painted symbols seemed to tell a story I couldn't decipher.

Rustin shrugged. "I've never seen workings like these. But I don't think so. If I had to guess, I'd say somebody was trying to get out of here."

I felt my eyes go wide. "Lea?"

Sebille shrugged. "Maybe. Have you found her and Hex?"

"We talked to her. But she still doesn't remember who she is," Grym said.

"And there's an older man who lives up the street from her," I told the sprite and the ghost witch. "He seems to know about the artifact. He was shooting at it."

"Shooting at it?" Rustin shook his head. "Sounds looney to me."

"He is a little," I admitted. "But you'd be crazy too if you had to live here for very long."

"Do you think you can figure out how to make this work?" I asked Rustin, pointing to the unknown spell.

"I can try. But my magic doesn't seem to work here in Mayberry," he said, frowning.

Grym nodded. "Mine either."

I looked at Sebille, feeling my stomach twist with alarm. "Please tell me yours works, sprite."

She shook her head. "Sorry, Naida."

I looked at Hobs, realizing that he hadn't used

his super-sonic speed since he'd been inside the artifact.

I took a deep breath and lifted my hand, sending a ribbon of keeper magic out into the universe.

For a moment, nothing happened. Then the most goddess-awful noise flared through the otherwise quiet spot. It sounded like an air-raid siren set on stun.

I doubled over, covering my ears with my hands and trying to make myself too small for the sound to find me. All around me, my friends hit the ground on their knees, no doubt doing the same thing.

Above our heads, dust bloomed from the country road, small rocks shooting off into the surrounding grass. Someone grabbed my arm, yanking me into the tunnel as the Sheriff's car flew past, going much faster than I'd thought it could go.

Inside the tunnel, the siren was like a physical force. Each wave of the appalling sound reverberated off the rounded concrete walls and seemed to get stuck there, slashing at my tortured eardrums until I thought I'd go mad.

Finally, the noise just stopped, the cessation almost more startling than the din had been.

I kept my hands over my ears for a few beats, just in case, and then cautiously let them slide away. "Is it over?"

"I think so." Grym's face was covered in a sheen

of sweat, his eyes looked haunted. "What was that about?"

I stared at my hand. "You don't think that was a reaction to my keeper magics, do you?"

"It could have been," Rustin said. "It seems more than likely, actually. And that means, when we get ready to try to take this thing down, we're going to have to move fast."

Horned hornet helmets! Just what we needed. More challenges.

"Miss!" Hobs' panicked voice brought my head up, and I started running through the tunnel.

"Now what?" Sebille groused behind me as I took off.

The tunnel was cool and dim, its smooth sides covered in brightly-hued drawings and symbols that made no sense to my scanning gaze. The ground was littered with debris too. A fact that made it seem out of place with the unnatural tidiness of the rest of the place. And there was an underlying stench of something sour. But I couldn't quite place what it was.

Overall, the tunnel was an unpleasant spot within the artifact, and one I was relieved to leave behind as I stepped out into the bright sunshine.

Until I saw what waited beyond the tunnel.

11

FLOUNDERING FISH FLIPPERS!

T he man's hair was an untidy dark spray on his round head, and his pale cotton button-up shirt was stained and rumpled above slacks that were just as untidy as the shirt.

He held Hobs effortlessly in one hand, despite the fact that he wavered on his feet, and his eyes kept trying to cross. The little hobgoblin's enormous eyes were even bigger than usual, his spidery fingers clenching and unclenching with uncertainty and fear.

"Don't hurt him," I said, knowing even as I said the words how useless they were.

The man's bulbous nose was dark, veiny. He held a filleting knife in one hand, the eye-watering stench of dead fish wafting from the blade as he brandished it in my direction. All around our feet, in the pale, sandy soil of the pond area, fish scales caught the sun and speared the air with colorless fire. The silvery glint of the scales was pretty but did nothing to overcome the miasma of guts and other detritus of fish-cleaning from the area.

A slime-covered tree stump stuck out of the ground not too far away, next to a small camp fire. I realized the man with the filleting knife probably caught, cleaned, and cooked his own dinner more often than not.

"Who are you people? You're not from around here." The words were spoken with the heat and force of an accusation. As if we were a band of mass murderers come to slaughter all his loved ones.

Grym moved carefully up behind me and lifted his hands. "We're friends. We don't want to hurt anybody."

"Liar!" said the man, his slightly bulgy gaze taking on a fanatic's gleam. The knife found its way to Hobs' throat, the meaty fist that was clutching it tensing as he pressed it close. "Y'all are up to no good. I can feel it in the air around you. There's buzzing. It feels dangerous and makes my skin prickle with gooseflesh."

Well, that was oddly specific.

I shook my head. "No! We're just trying to find our friends. We'll find them and go. You'll never see us again. I promise."

The man shook his head. "It don't work that way and you know it." He lifted the knife away from

Hobs' throat, swinging it wildly in front of his own face and nearly slicing off his veiny nose. His movement was manic, his gaze wild. "Stop it! Stop the buzzing."

I wanted to share a look with Grym but I was afraid to look away from Hobs. The man was clearly beyond crazy. He was being affected by something that was causing his mind to shift. And I hoped it wasn't us. I thought of Sebille's phone.

Could that be it?

"We can help," Grym said gently, taking a small step forward. "Whatever's making your skin crawl, we can help you with it. We just need you to tell us how? How can we help?"

The man shook his head, swinging his knife-wielding hand through the air and nearly stabbing Hobs with the stinky blade in the process.

The little hobgoblin yelped softly, trying to duck away from the wildly flailing blade but unable to go anywhere with the man's meaty fist dug into his shirt.

Something moved, low on the ground, drawing my gaze.

Wicked!

My cat sauntered toward the madman as if he were greeting a visitor in Croakies. Calm as you please, tail dancing gently on the air behind him, Wicked rubbed against the man's ankle, his fur brushing the bare and filthy skin I could see above the stranger's sockless shoes.

The man twitched once and then looked down.

I moved before he could slash at Wicked with the knife.

But Grym was faster.

He jumped the man, throwing him to the ground and knocking the knife from his fist even as Hobs spun safely away.

The hobgoblin didn't waste any time getting out of the man's reach. He flew toward Sebille and jumped into her arms, wrapping his long arms and legs around her and burying his face in her shoulder.

"Shh, it's okay, buddy," Sebille crooned.

"Is he okay?" I asked.

She nodded.

Grym tugged the guy to his feet, and I kicked the knife away. "What's your name?" the cop asked him.

The man had deflated as soon as Grym got hold of him, his shoulders sagging as he lowered his head. "I'm Otis. I don't want to hurt nobody."

"Why did you try to hurt our friend?" I asked.

He shook his head, pointing toward the tunnel. "Nobody's allowed in there. That's my bridge."

I frowned, catching Grym's eye over Otis's bowed head. "You live under the bridge?"

Otis rubbed his face with his free hand. "I don't belong. Never belong. Never."

Rustin came up next to me. "Are these your drawings?" Rustin asked the man.

Otis looked at the symbols. "It's my work. I have to do my work." He shook his head, shuddering violently. "Something's wrong. Something's buzzing. It's buzzing around you."

I narrowed my gaze at Sebille and she cringed.

It was her cell phone. It had to be. And if Otis was so sensitive that he'd felt it from clear across the road, I doubted flinging it into the pond was going to be enough to neutralize its effects. "We're sorry we bothered you, Otis," I told the man. "We'll be gone soon."

He shook his head. "Nobody goes. They'll feel the buzzing. Nobody goes. They'll feel the buzzing."

Ice covered my spine at his words. If he was right, then we were in deep trouble. Because we might have found all our friends, but we were still a long way from finding a way back home.

And it sounded as if we'd just run out of time.

I heard an engine on the road again and looked up to find the Sheriff's car returning, driving slowly as if searching for someone.

For us.

Both lawmen were inside the car.

"We need to get out of here," Grym said. "They're going to find us if we don't go somewhere else."

Otis swung a big hand in front of his face. "Buzzing, buzzing. Need to hide from the buzzing."

I wrinkled my nose at the alcoholic stench coming from the other man. It was as if it came from his pores rather than his mouth.

"Where can we hide, Otis?" Sebille asked.

The man just shook his head and continued swatting the air.

Hobs lifted his head. "In the tunnel."

It was all we had. There was no time to find anything else. But it seemed like pretty weak cover. All the bumpkin cops would have to do is stop the car and walk down the embankment to find us.

"Let's go!" Grym said, herding us all toward the cool dimness beneath the road.

"What about him?" Rustin asked, pointing at Otis.

"We need to bring him with us," I told Grym. "If Fiff or the Sheriff see him standing here all agitated, they might come to investigate."

Grym grabbed Otis's beefy arm and pulled him into the tunnel with us.

Dread slid over me again as we stepped into the culvert, but I soon forgot it as the police car approached. The oversized car drove slowly up to the overpass, seeming to slow to a crawl, and then eased to a stop above our heads.

We huddled together beneath the cool concrete, barely breathing as, first one car door and then another creaked open above us.

"You reckon they're around here somwheres, Andrew?"

I recognized Deputy Fiff's reedy tone and held my breath, praying to the goddess they didn't come exploring.

"I reckon they is, Barney. Ain't noplace else to hide in these parts. And I'm plum certain that siren come from here." The Sheriff's voice was deeper than Fiff's, the tone filled with harmless interest. But I could feel the razor edge beneath it and knew the "good old boy" thing was all an act.

Hobs slid out of Sebille's arms and crouched in front of her, his eyes wide enough to pop out of his head.

I eyed him, frowning a warning.

He twitched backward, sliding behind Sebille again, and inadvertently kicked a stone.

It flew across the tunnel and clanged against the concrete wall across from us, reverberating through the tunnel.

We all tensed as, above us, the two men fell silent.

"What was that?" Barney asked, his shrill voice deepening to a threatening tone.

"I don't know, Barney, but I reckon I'm gonna find out."

My grip tightened on my cat as footsteps started down the bank at the side of the road. Rocks skittered down with their steps, each one seeming to ping against my nerves like notes on a badly tuned violin.

I shared a look with Grym and he sighed. The jig was up. We needed to face the music...erm...Sheriff.

Without warning, Wicked jumped from my arms. He trotted toward the opening of the culvert, tail high and whipping the air.

"Wicked, no!" I whispered.

My cat ignored me as only he can do.

Grym grabbed my arm to stop me when I would have gone after him.

"Well, lookee here, Andrew," Fiff said. "It's Thelma Lou's cat. What in the world do you suppose she's doin' here?"

"No idea, Deputy. But I reckon cats like ta wander." There was a beat of silence before the Sheriff went on. "How's our Thelma doin', Barney. She fittin' in okay?"

I tensed, realizing they were discussing whether they needed to be worried about Lea.

"She's right as rain, Sheriff. You got no cause ta worry about that gal. She's madly in love with yours truly."

"Well, just keep an eye on her, Barn. I'm a bit worried about the timin' of her arrival here at Mayberry. She come just about the same time as those circus people. If she starts actin' off, you know what we'll need ta do. Ain't no room for rabble-rousers in Mayberry."

Ice formed in my belly at his words. Lea seemed to be struggling. If they interpreted that as a threat, she could be in real danger.

Rocks crunched and I pictured the Sheriff crouching down to pet my cat. "Hey, gal. You best get on back home now. They's things about that ain't healthy for good folk."

"Meow!"

"Awe, ain't she a nice kitty. Get on now."

Wicked shot away from the culvert and we watched him trot toward the playground in the distance. I prayed they didn't notice that Wicked was a male cat.

"Let's go, Barney. I want to drive through town again. Those varmints have to be here somewhere and I'm fixin' ta find 'em."

As soon as the car had turned around and headed back to town, I started off after my cat. "We need to check on Lea. I didn't like the sound of that Sheriff's interest in her."

"What do you suppose they do to, rabble-rousers?" Sebille asked, frowning.

"Nothing good, I'm sure," Rustin responded.

We were nearly out of the tunnel before Grym whistled. We all stopped, turning back to find him with Otis still in hand. "What are we going to do with him?"

I frowned, realizing we couldn't just leave him

there. He might talk to the Sheriff about us. I sighed. "I guess he'll have to come with us."

It was less than ideal. Otis was dead weight, and unpredictable at best. But I did feel a little guilty about making him go all cray-cray. Or at least Sebille and her phone had.

Maybe, if we brought him along, we could figure out how to help him with the buzzing he was hearing.

Or, at least, show him how to play Angry Sparrows on the thing, so he'd be distracted.

Lea wasn't home when we got there. Her house was empty, and her doors were unlocked. I tried not to panic about the unlocked doors thing. It was the kind of thing people who'd lived in the country in the 60s had probably done. But, since I knew the Sheriff was keeping an eye on her, not knowing where she'd gone was concerning.

We settled in to await her arrival back at the house. I knew it would be hard to explain our presence there. I also knew it would probably cause my friend undue worry to find the entire motley crew sitting in her kitchen. But I'd made a decision. We needed to get Lca on our side fast. We'd inadvertently pinned a giant target on our backs and I was afraid she was going to be targeted with us.

Ignorance had just become too dangerous for her.

12

SEE? HE'S FINE. WE NEED TO GET OUT OF HERE

While we waited, Hobs perused the refrigerator, complaining that he was hungry. I was hungry too, though I'd been trying to ignore the aching hole in my belly since we'd arrived. I didn't want to take time to eat. I'd rather do what we'd come to do and get the heck out of Dodge...er...Mayberry.

But it seemed we weren't going anywhere very fast. So I stood up and joined him in front of the old-fashioned rounded refrigerator. It was so small compared to modern fridges, and so empty. "She has no food." I frowned. "How can she have no food?" I really wished the rest of that chocolate cake was there. It had looked delicious.

Sebille opened cabinets and one small closet looking for food and found nothing. "It's like the abyss, where everything's just for show."

"No food," Otis mumbled, shaking his head. "Don't drink the water. Don't eat the food."

I felt my eyes go wide. "Does the food and water do something to you?" I asked the distraught man.

Otis swung a hand in front of his face. "Buzzing."

"It's probably safer not to eat the food or drink the water if we can help it," Rustin said, frowning.

As soon as he said the words, my stomach twisted in pain. I was starving. Nausea bloomed as I realized I wasn't going to be able to eat.

I was going to die!

It could be that I was suffering from a bit of hunger hysteria. It happened occasionally.

Okay, full disclosure, it happened every time I realized it was going to be more than a few minutes before I ate again.

Hobs had given up on the refrigerator and was sitting at the table. It took me only a minute to notice the glossy coating around his lips. He stopped chewing when I spotted him, his eyes going wide.

"Hobs? What are you eating?"

He shook his head, his eyes like golf balls in his head.

"Hobs?"

Grym leaned over and snatched something from the hobgoblin's lap, holding it up for us to see. "Look familiar?"

It was the artifact I'd brought from home. The

never-ending slice of pie artifact. It had returned from Aberdeen's place.

The glossy dregs of a slice of cherry pie was all that was left there, but as we watched, another slice of pie began to form on the pretty, china plate.

Coconut cream!

Looking at it, my mouth watered. "That smells delicious."

We all stared lustfully at the plate, licking our lips.

"That's not from here, though," Sebille said after a moment. "It should be safe, right?"

I hoped so, because Hobs and I had already eaten from it. I grimaced at the thought, shrugging.

Suddenly, Grym reached out and snagged the slice of pie, shoving the endpoint into his mouth and eating a third of it in one bite.

"Hey!" we exclaimed.

He closed his eyes on a moan. "So good," he said, buttery pastry crumbs shooting out of his mouth.

Another slice formed on the plate. I grabbed it.

Two minutes later, we all had a slice and Hobs was eating his second.

Wicked trotted in, yowling unhappily and I gave him a chunk of my banana cream slice.

I was scraping whipped cream off my nose when Lea walked into her own kitchen, a paper bag held in her arms and her eyes wide.

We all stopped mid-chew, looking guilty.

"Umph..." I started to say, snagging an errant crumb with my fingertip before it escaped my mouth.

"What are you doing here? Is that pie?" She glared at me as if I were the only culprit, but I didn't miss the way her eyes slid hopefully to the triangle of pie in my hand.

I swallowed hard. "Lea, I mean Thelma, you need to eat some of this pie."

She shook her head, forcing her gaze from the slice. "I...I'm on a diet."

Dangling duck doodles! The witch's diets were going to be the end of her. Literally.

My plea turned to inspiration. If Lea were sitting on the razor edge of confused, maybe eating pie from a plate that had come from home would fix her. "I must insist," I told her, grabbing the plate and advancing on her with a glossy slice of chocolate meringue.

She shook her head and stepped back, dropping her bag. "I don't want it!"

"It's sugar-free!" yelled Sebille, apparently picking up on the same thought I'd had.

"You're beautiful just like you are," Rustin added, earning an odd look from...well...all of us. He shrugged. "It's true."

I forced myself to stop chasing her across the room. "Thelma, I'll be honest. This pie will be good for you."

She blinked, staring at the pie like a woman who'd lived on a desert island without food for a week. "It will?"

"Yes. Chocolate is medicinal. And you look like you really need it."

That wasn't a lie. And, I was pretty sure chocolate *was* medicinal. It certainly was for me.

When she still hesitated, Hobs reached his long fingers toward the plate. "She doesn't want it, Miss…"

Quick as a snake, Lea growled, diving on the slice of pie. She turned to Hobs and hissed. "Mine!"

Whoa, girl!

We all backed up a step and waited as Lea eased it gently between her lips. A moment later, she was licking chocolate from her fingers, her eyes closed in pleasure.

I offered her another slice. She snatched at it, taking the whole plate.

Five minutes later, she settled the plate on the table and fell into a chair, groaning. "I was so hungry."

"You went to the grocery?" Sebille asked, picking up the discarded bag and looking inside.

Lea shook her head. "The drug store. There's a new pharmacist. She's pretty, but there's something in her eyes that makes me uncomfortable." She frowned. "There doesn't seem to be a grocery. There's only a diner downtown. I…" She frowned. "I might have eaten there once. But everything's a blur."

We shared a look. I knew somebody had to ask, but I was afraid to know if the pie had worked. Finally, when it seemed no one else was going to do it, I asked, "Lea?"

She laid her head back, her eyes still closed. "Hmm?"

Joy filled me.

Then her eyes shot open and she fixed them on Sebille. "What in the world are you wearing?" She frowned. "And who are you?" She sat up again, waving her arms around the room. "What are you all doing in my kitchen?" Her gaze fell on Otis. "Oh, hi Otis. How are you?"

His only response was to swat the air in front of his face.

She sighed. Spotting Wicked, she reached out and tugged him off the table, burying her face in his fur. After a beat, she pulled him away and frowned. "You're not Hex."

Wicked rubbed his head under her chin. "Meow!"

"That's Wicked," I said. I pointed to Hobs. "That's Hobs, he's a..."

"Hobgoblin," Lea murmured. She looked at Grym. "You're Grym."

He nodded and I felt a spurt of excitement. But then I remembered she'd met Grym earlier.

She stared at the ghost witch for a beat. "You have a dragon. An amalgamate."

Hope flared.

"I do. Sadie. She wanted to come, but it was too dangerous."

Lea nodded. "Color is energy for them." She lifted her brows at Sebille. "You know, you look like a circus freak in this town."

Sebille rolled her eyes. "Don't be a shrew, witch. We gave you pie."

Lea chuckled. "You guys, that was scary. I didn't know who I was." She wrinkled her pert nose. "This place is *weird*!"

And with a squeal of pure pleasure, I threw myself at her.

***

Heavy, insistent pounding shook Lea's front door.

We all stilled and turned our gazes toward the front door, past the gray couch, darker gray chairs, and the table with the vase of colorless flowers.

I looked at Lea. "Were you expecting someone?"

She laughed. "I wasn't expecting *you*, and yet here you are."

She had a point.

"Yeah, but it was a happy surprise, right?"

Lea grinned. "I got pie out of it." She started for the door. "Stay back just in case it's...you know anybody who wants to turn you permanently gray."

We all dodged out of sight, peering into the living room as Lea opened the fake-wood-grained front door.

A man pushed past Lea and hurried into the room, his hair a disheveled mess.

Hex trotted in on Old Mr. Aberdeen's heels.

One of them was still dressed just in his underwear.

Lea eyed the old man's outfit. "Well, at least you added boots."

And he had. Combat style, with saggy cotton socks drooping on his skinny calves. "You're in danger, Lass."

Lass? I mouthed at the sprite. She lifted her brows, her gray freckles dancing in surprise.

Lea scooped up her cat. "I'm glad to see you. I was getting worried."

"Thanks, but I can take care of myself," Aberdeen responded.

Lea looked as if she was considering telling the man she hadn't been talking to him and then apparently changed her mind. "What's going on?"

"You need to come with me. Things are coming to a head, and you're not safe here anymore."

"What do you mean they're coming to a head?"

The old man expelled a gusty breath. "Don't be difficult now, Lass. This is serious!"

Her front door opened again and two more men came in. They had chin-length black hair, mean faces, and black eyes.

I grabbed Grym's wrist. "Wizards!" I said in a harsh whisper.

"Who was that?" one of the wizards demanded as he strode toward us, something long and pointy in his hands.

The sprite sprang.

Okay, that was fun.

The sprite sprang.

Yep, still fun.

She stood like a throwing star in front of the door, a...fork clutched in her hand. "Don't come any closer!"

The Wizard looked at the fork, then at Sebille's socks, and laughed. "Is the circus in town?"

Sebille glowered.

"Oh good, you're here!" said the crazy man in his underwear. "You all need to come with us."

Grym stepped up behind Sebille, adding his glower to hers and thereby layering on the threat. "Not until you tell us what's going on."

"What do you think's goin' on boyo? We're bustin' out of this joint."

"Why is Old Mr. Aberdeen talking funny?" I whispered to Sebille.

She rolled her eyes.

"Busting out of what joint?" Grym asked, his glower softening.

"Don't be stupid!" Aberdeen bellowed.

"Shut up, old man!" The wizard closest to the door said. "*They're* gonna hear you."

"Tell us what's going on!" Lea demanded,

Wicked slipped through our legs and trotted out into the living room. He stopped a few feet away from the wizards and hissed, the hair on his back lifting.

"We'll explain once we get there," the first wizard said, eyeing my cat.

I shook my head. "Not a chance. We don't trust wizards. You either tell us now, or we stay here."

"Let's just leave, 'em!" the first wizard suggested from his spot in front of the door. He had his eye to the crack and seemed to be lookout for the mangy operation.

Aberdeen scrubbed a big hand through his wild mop of hair. "Okay, the short version is this. Like you, we were pulled into this goddess-forsaken place against our will. We've been tryin' to get out for years. We're gettin' closer and the thing is gettin' a little peevish from our efforts. It's no longer safe to be out here. We're goin' into hidin', and we think you should come with us since it knows you're here and you're not fittin' in."

"How much time do we have?" Rustin asked.

The front yard exploded, blowing the front door inside and sweeping the wizard on watch inside with it. He skidded across the gray carpet and slammed into the wall, inches from where we stood.

Aberdeen and the other wizard hit their knees, covering their heads as bits of Lea's furniture pummeled them.

"That answers that," Grym yelled. "Let's go!"

Grym helped Aberdeen to his feet, and we started for the front door. Another explosion mere feet from the house convinced us we needed to go out the back.

"Hurry!" the first wizard said. "Things change fast here."

I had no idea what he was suggesting until I noticed the back door shrinking away. The kitchen was darker than it should have been, and I realized the windows were already gone, replaced by more walls and cabinets.

By the time we reached it, the door was six inches off the ground and only about eighteen inches wide. Hobs, Sebille, and Rustin jumped through, quickly followed by the two cats. Grym made me go next and then shoved Otis and Aberdeen through.

The wizards shoved Grym aside and jumped through as the door continued to shrink. I screamed, seeing Grym's face disappearing behind the closing door.

"Festering frog farts!" I screamed, grabbing Sebille's fork and repeatedly stabbing the stupid wizards with it.

"Ow! You flaming gnack!"

Aberdeen grabbed the wizard's pointy stick before he could hit me with it.

"Come on," Lea yelled. "There's a window in the bedroom."

We hurried around just in time to see that window disappear with a pop. The window on the other end of the small house was already gone.

"Grym's trapped! I wailed.

"Not quite," Rustin said. "The front door is still open."

As he spoke, a third explosion shook the ground.

"And under attack," I said. "We need a distraction."

Sebille sighed. "I guess it's time for the circus to open for business. She looked at Hobs. You in?"

Hobs grinned wildly. He grabbed a small, pink bicycle that lay forgotten in the grass of the house next door and climbed on, sounding the horn as he took off around the house, handle streamers jauntily flying.

Sebille ran after him.

"We're out of here," the wizards said and took off running.

Aberdeen glared after then. "I really hate those guys."

"Come on!" I said. We took off running around the opposite end of the house. By the time we reached the front corner, I was dismayed to find an unleapable crater in front of the blasted-out door.

Adding to our challenges, the front of the house had caught fire and smoke was pouring out into the yard.

"The big window," Lea said as another missile was lobbed from the gray, roiling sky.

The jaunty sound of a horn brought our gazes around to where Hobs rode the tiny pink bike down to the sidewalk, Sebille doing...cartwheels...alongside him?

What in the goddesses favorite sparkly reading glasses was that all about?

"Did you know Sebille could do cartwheels?" Lea whispered to me.

"Not a clue," I said, thinking that, if we lived through the current mess, I was going to blackmail her with it for the rest of my days.

"And a roundhouse," Rustin said, grinning.

Insistent knocking brought our attention back to the problem at hand. Grym was inside the big window, pounding on the glass. "It won't open," he yelled. "See if you can break it."

We looked around for anything we could throw at the window, praying the clown show on the sidewalk would keep the hostile artifact distracted long enough for us to figure out how to break it.

Rustin came up with a really big rock. He threw it at the glass and it pinged off, leaving only a divot behind in the window.

"What the heck is that window made out of?" Lea groused.

The ground rumbled slightly, and we jerked our heads around to find Hobs and Sebille making a run for it as another missile sailed toward them from the sky. They dove behind a tree as the missile hit, signaling an end to the distraction portion of our entertainment.

We threw several more large rocks at the window with no luck.

"I wish I had my shotgun with me," Aberdeen lamented.

"There's only one thing we can do," I told my friends. "Take cover."

"What do you have in mind?" Rustin asked, frowning.

"Get behind something," I yelled to Grym. "Take cover!"

He nodded and disappeared. Taking a deep breath, I moved out of the bushes and stood in plain sight, waving my arms. "Hey, big ugly! Over here!"

A silvery star blossomed in the gray clouds, shooting toward the ground on a trail of fire and smoke. I realized pretty quickly that they were right on target. If I didn't move fast, there was going to be a whole lot more of me on the ground.

"Naida!" Lea screamed.

I turned and ran as the magic missile whistled through the air, the heat it generated preceding it by several dozen feet.

I leaped off the ground and hit the area behind a massive tree as the missile slammed into the earth, sending dirt and chunks of wood and glass into the air in a deadly spray.

Aberdeen grunted as I landed on him, one of his bony knees finding my soft underbelly and knocking the wind out of me.

An eerie silence followed the hit. A silence fraught with hesitation, as if the artifact was waiting to see if it got us.

Smoke hung thick in the air as the broken building settled with a groan and glass tinkled musically to the ground. I shoved to a sitting position and looked on with horror as I caught a glimpse of what was left of Lea's house.

The front was a gaping wound, engulfed in flames.

"Grym," I whispered in horror.

Rustin grabbed my arm. "We have to move, Naida."

I shook my head, tears sliding down my cheeks. "I killed him."

The smoke shifted and what was left of the window crashed to the ground, sparks spitting from its pocked surface. A beat later, an enormous figure slid through the hole to the debris-strewn ground.

He lumbered toward us, smoke wreathing the entire top half of his frame.

"See? He's fine," Rustin said. "Come on, we need to get out of here."

13

AN EVIL KIND OF DELIGHT

I threw myself at Grym. "I'm so sorry! It was all I could think of to do."

Grym wrapped his arms around me, holding me so tight it constricted my lungs. A tiny spark flared on the shoulder of his shirt and I smacked it down with the palm of my hand. Smoke wafted around us, creating a cocoon that turned Grym's hug to something I hadn't expected.

As if he'd felt the change too, Grym lifted his head and looked down at me, his usually warm caramel gaze made inscrutable through the haze.

We stared at each other for several beats, something coiling warm and interesting in my belly, and then the smoke burst apart and a hand snaked through, grabbing my arm. "Come on, Naida!" Sebille ground out, yanking me out of Grym's arms. "We need to move now!"

I reluctantly turned away from Grym, trudging along behind the sprite as she hurried around the corner and we caught up with the others.

"Follow me," Aberdeen said. He hobbled through the smoky air, his big boots clomping against the ground and his wispy gray hair floating around his head. We kept to the smoke for as long as we could, though we were all choking from it by the time we stepped out of Lea's yard.

It had been good cover and, when we took off running across the open grass leading to the little playground down the street, I felt exposed and vulnerable.

My gaze kept sliding toward the sky, where clouds still roiled angrily high above us. The gods of the artifact world were still agitated.

That wasn't good for us.

Aberdeen reached the merry-go-round and stepped onto its wobbly surface, grabbing a curved handle in the center as it moved out from underneath him. He motioned frantically for us to join him.

I stared at the play structure, frowning. "What are you doing? This is no time to play."

The guy truly was crazy.

Aberdeen shook his head. "Just do as I tell you to. Hurry. I feel something in the air."

He was right. As soon as he said the words, I realized the pressure was building again. Whatever had pelted us from the clouds before was gearing up to do it again. With no better ideas myself, I stepped onto the merry-go-round with the others. Aberdeen nodded toward the cats. "Somebody had better hold them."

"Why?" I asked, reaching for Wicked.

Lea bent to pick up Hex just as the structure began to move.

"Hold on!" Aberdeen said.

As if his voice had called for more attacks, the ground a mere ten feet away exploded upward, sending dirt and rock into the air above our heads.

We covered our heads as best we could while still holding onto the structure. Grym grabbed the handles on either side of Wicked and me and bent over us as hard clumps of dusty dirt pinged against the pocked metal surface.

And then I no longer noticed the falling debris. Because the world had begun to spin fast enough to pull the breath right out of my lungs. And my stomach smacked up against my spine.

It seemed to go on forever, and when it finally slowed, we were in a different place entirely.

In fact, for a moment, I thought maybe we'd gone back home.

The structure squealed to a stop and we all stood there, eyes half-wild as our bodies adjusted to the sudden stillness after being literally whipped into a frenzy.

We were standing in some kind of a massive room with concrete floors and dark walls covered in cloth. There were no visible windows and the only lighting was spare. Small lights arrayed along the floor, seemingly only geared toward keeping someone from walking into things, not really meant to illuminate.

Enormous shapes surrounded us, bent and misshapen objects that I couldn't identify. And across the large building, three-walled, open film sets dotted the space.

I recognized the Sheriff's Office from Andrew of Mayberry as one of the sets. And next to it down a short distance, was an old western town, complete with two horses whose reins had been thrown over a tie bar in front of the faux buildings. The equine heads were lowered and their jaws busily churned through the hay someone had provided at their feet.

A man lounged in a wooden rocking chair near the horses, a long piece of grass dangling from between his lips. I recognized Otis. He must have left Lea's with the wizards. He stared calmly in our direction. No longer seeming bothered by the buzzing he'd been driven nearly mad by before.

"Where are we?" I asked Aberdeen.

He walked away from us, heading toward Otis with a wave for us to follow. "Come on. I'll introduce you around."

We followed him through a pair of swinging

doors in the building where Otis lounged, into what looked like a Saloon.

Otis silently stood as we filed inside and brought up the rear.

Aberdeen was waiting for us at the front of a small group of people. He nodded toward the two wizards standing nearby. "You've met Wiz and Zane."

We all nodded a

t the two supernormals.

"And Otis," Aberdeen said, pointing to the man leaning against the door frame.

Otis scanned a slightly hostile look over us.

"Let me formally introduce myself," Aberdeen said. "My name is McDonald. You can call me Dugan."

I felt my eyes go wide. "You're Mrs. Foxladle's friend?"

He nodded. "Nice lady. She told you about me?"

"Mrs. F told Naida about the television artifact," Grym said, frowning. "When she and Sebille went to collect it, they discovered you were missing." He cocked his head. "You're not human, are you?"

Dugan laughed. "Leprechaun." He did a little dance, earning himself a pair of rolled eyes from Wiz and Zane.

I scanned a look over the rest, recognizing the short, rounded physique of a gnome and a man whose unusual hairiness probably meant he was some kind of shifter.

Aberdeen pointed to the gnome. "That's Alec."

Alec the Gnome waved in our direction.

"And Peter." He grinned. "Wolf shifter."

"Peter Wolf?" Grym asked, his expression amused.

Peter shrugged. "What can I tell you, my parents had a sense of humor."

Rustin crossed his arms over his chest. "We're all supernormals."

I blinked. He was right. "This artifact only pulls supernormals inside?"

Aberdeen, er, Dugan, nodded. "And it only keeps the ones who it can force to assimilate. These other poor schlubs you see moving around the place have totally lost themselves to the world. They likely don't even remember ever being outside."

A keen sense of sadness filled me at the thought. I glanced at Lea and found her frowning. She'd been heading in that direction herself. Thank goodness I'd had the never-ending pie artifact. Which made me wonder aloud. "How?"

Dugan looked at me, a question in his light-gray gaze.

"How do they make people assimilate so completely? And why haven't you all done it?"

"Food," Alec responded. "The only food they

provide is at the diner. Everyone who eats at the diner is slowly poisoned into forgetting."

I looked at Lea. "You think you ate there?"

She looked as if she was trying to remember. "I think I might have once or twice over the last couple of weeks."

Time clearly passed very differently in Mayberry. Lea clearly perceived her time in faux Mayberry as having been a lot longer than the few hours I'd experienced.

"But how have you survived?" Rustin asked the small group.

"By hook or by crook," Dugan said. "Our magic actually works some in this hidden space. Only a very limited amount. We've basically given up using it except to create food and water to survive while we try to find a way out of here."

"The fish in the pond are safe," Otis added from behind me. "We eat those."

I glanced at him, understanding blossoming. Suddenly the filleting knife and all the fish parts littering the area around the culvert made total sense.

I swung my arm around. "What is this place?"

"The Behind the Scenes," Alec said, grinning. "It's beyond everyone's notice because it's inherently outside of the reality they know."

"We have some leeway here," Dugan said. "Being

invisible is part of that. Having limited power is another part."

I thought of the never-ending pie plate and wondered where it had gotten to. Had it been blown up in Lea's house? I could call it back to me, but I wasn't sure that was such a good idea. "I tried to use my keeper magics outside and it made a horrendous noise," I told them.

Dugan winced. "Yeah. We heard."

"Just about scared the troll to death," Alec said. "It took him right back to his feral roots for a while."

They all glanced at Otis and I had an "Ah ha!" moment. A bridge troll. No wonder he'd claimed the culvert and painted it with symbols. "He's been trying to make a bridge out of here, hasn't he?"

Dugan nodded.

Flushing with embarrassment, I asked, "Do you think my magic would do the same thing here?"

Shrugging, Wiz said, "None of our magics make that kind of ruckus. "They either work or they don't. No fuss. No noise."

"Naida's magic is intrinsically dangerous to this artifact," Lea said. "There are apparently protections against it."

We fell silent, everyone probably thinking over the possibilities and limitations that information implied.

"We'll need to make sure we're ready to move before we risk her using it then," Peter said.

"What exactly do you have in mind?" Grym asked.

"We need to find the heart of the artifact," Dugan said. "The heart is the key."

"The heart?" Lea asked, frowning. "Like a real, beating heart?"

They shrugged. "We're not sure. We've been trying to figure that out but haven't had much luck so far," Otis said from behind us.

"That's where we were hoping you could help," Dugan said. "We thought maybe you could use your keeper energies to locate the thing's heart. But if you can't use them without creating an end of the world scenario..." He shook his head, looking defeated.

"Someone has to know where the heart is," Rustin said. "It might be buried in the collective memory somewhere. Maybe all we need to do is ask."

They looked surprised at the idea.

The simplest solution is sometimes the last one anybody considers.

"Do you really think they'll tell us?" asked Zane petulantly.

Rustin shrugged. "It's worth a shot."

"But who's going to ask them?" Dugan asked, frowning. "They know all of us on sight."

I looked around at my friends. "Lea's out, she's been too high profile, and they might believe she's turned on them at this point." The attack at her home no doubt indicated that. "Grym and I are out for the same reason."

Rustin winced. "I'm afraid I might have painted a target on myself in town."

"What did you do?" Grym asked.

Sebille sighed. "It was my fault. Some little old lady came up to me and started to tell me about all her aches and pains, and I told her I didn't care and to get lost."

Compassion, thy name is NOT Sebille, I thought, grinning.

"The old lady stood in the middle of the street and kept grabbing my arm to tell me about some pain that went all the way down her back, over her hip and down her leg," Sebille appeared thoroughly disgusted. "I told her I had no idea why she was telling a complete stranger about her imaginary pains and that if she didn't stop hanging out in the middle of the road she was going to have some real pains to worry about."

"Emma," the entire Behind-the-Scenes group said in unison, nodding their heads knowingly.

"Oh Sebille," I said, fighting a smile.

Sebille shrugged. "That old woman threatened to hit me over the head with her purse."

"So far it sounds as if *you* were the problem, not Rustin," Grym said.

Rustin grimaced. "Yeah. It *was* her up until the

next minute. I kind of...accidentally...hit the old lady with her own purse."

I felt my eyes go wide. "You what!?"

Sebille snorted.

"It was an accident," he insisted. "I grabbed the purse to keep her from hitting Sebille with it and somebody started screaming, Thief! Thief! behind me. When I whipped around to deny it, the purse accidentally hit the old lady in the belly. She made this breathless kind of 'ugh!' sound and started toppling toward the ground."

Wiz and Zane were hysterical by this point in Rustin's story, holding onto each other to keep from falling down.

Dugan glared at Rustin. "You struck Emma? She's just a harmless little old woman."

Rustin frowned. "Yeah, well, the big guy running after me with the baseball bat wasn't harmless or little."

I covered my mouth to hide a grin. "What did you do?"

"I ran!" he said as if I were totally stupid. He glared over at the sprite. "Of course, Sebille was nowhere to be seen at that point. Nobody even remembered she'd been the one to start the fight."

"I didn't start the fight," Sebille objected with clear outrage. "The old lady did."

Rustin just shook his head.

"*That's* why you were hiding out by the culvert?" I asked, appalled.

Rustin looked ashamed. The sprite was high-fiving the wizards.

"Let me see if I have this straight," Lea said, her lips twitching. "We're considering putting *Sebille* out there to speak to...people?"

Sebille glared over at her. "I can people if I have to."

"Clearly," Alec said, snorting out a laugh.

"Look," the sprite said in a weak, very belated defense of her own actions. "I'm not a compassionate person. People who know me know this. But if I'm going to be asking about the heart of Mayberry, that's not a good segway to, 'Look at this hairy wart on my left big toe.'" She nodded as if that made perfect sense. "Ergo, I'll have no reason to punch anybody. It'll be fine."

Nobody else looked convinced. But I sighed. I didn't see that we had much choice. "Okay. So how do we want to play this?"

"Easy," Grym said. "She's a reporter from the big city, come to town to find out how the rural half lives."

Lea frowned. "*Which* big city?"

We all looked around. Nobody had any idea where Mayberry was supposed to be. Finally, Dugan said. "It won't matter, lass. All ya have ta say is the

Big City. These folks aren't used ta askin' a lot of questions."

"Fine," I said, feeling as if it were anything but fine. "Let's get her ready to play the part."

Sebille's eyes went wide. "Ready? I'm ready now. What do you mean, get me ready?"

I let my lips turn up in an evil grin, just to tweak her a little. I told myself I was doing it to pay her back for being mean to sweet old Emma. But I strongly suspected it was really because I could. And because it gave me an evil kind of delight.

14

ME AND MY PARDNER ARE LOOKIN' TO
WET OUR WHISTLES

Sebille clung to the pristine brick of the alley wall. Her light gray eyes were huge and fathomless behind the thick glass of the wire-rimmed spectacles. The cotton dress had a tab collar and short sleeves with cuffs that jutted out in points from her skinny arms. I'd never seen Sebille's arms before. As far as I knew, she'd only ever worn sleeves so long they usually covered her hands.

I could see why she covered them. They were spindly and pale, like balcony uprights that had been formed on a lathe.

But it wasn't the spindly bare arms that were the most entertaining...or horrific...depending on whether you were looking at it from Sebille's perspective or everybody else's. The dress fit her slim form tightly at the waist and then flared outward like a cloth explosion. It rounded away from her middle like a toadstool, stopping a few inches above the skinniest ankles I'd ever seen.

As far as I was concerned, the folded white cotton socks inside the Mary Jane shoes were just icing on the cake.

I gently shoved the sprite, putting a little muscle behind it as she continued to cling to the wall like a barnacle on a whale. "Come on, Sebille, time's wasting."

"I look ridiculous."

I bit back on the urge to agree, knowing it wouldn't help us get her out there any faster. "You look like you belong, which is a good thing."

She clutched the tiny notebook we'd dug up from Behind the Scenes and gave me a mulish look. "I think *you* should do this," she told me. "You're better at peopling than I am."

Nobody could deny it. However, that wasn't saying much. "We've already discussed this, Sebille..." Multiple times. "I've been burned. They've already pegged me as a hostile. You're it. You're all we've got. Now put your big girl bloomers on and get in there. And whatever you do, don't eat the food."

Sebille expelled a breath that almost blew me over with its intensity, and then whipped around the corner and headed for the *Mayberry Diner* half a block up.

I turned to Grym. "She's engaged."

He nodded and signaled to Wiz and Zane, who

were in charge of monitoring the cameras inside the diner.

I'd learned with horror that most of the buildings inside the artifact had cameras for interior shots. But the guys had assured me the ones at Lea's had been disabled, as had Dugan's. They'd sensed she might be a rebel like them and Dugan had been working on bringing her over.

Grym and I were supposed to stay close in case Sebille needed us, but Dugan, who'd been an electrical engineer before he retired, had rigged Sebille's illegal cell phone to work as another camera eye, thus taking it offline as far as the artifact was concerned — or online, depending on your perspective — and giving us an eagle-eye view into the diner.

We settled down into a little niche formed from a side door into the alley, watching as Sebille exploded into the diner as if someone had shot her from a gun. She stopped just inside the door, blinking like an owl behind the thick glasses.

"This is gonna be great," I told Grym. "I wonder if I can get a copy of this before we leave."

He shook his head, but his lips twitched and I knew he was enjoying it at least as much as I was.

The woman behind the counter looked up and smiled widely. "Hello. Sit wherever you'd like."

Sebille stood stiffly for a moment as if stymied by

the instruction, and then walked toward the counter. "I..."

The waitress wiped a damp cloth over the counter and raised perfectly sculpted eyebrows, waiting.

"I..."

The woman's smile dimmed. She shook her head. "Are you all right, honey? You look a little pale."

"Hehehe," I said.

Grym didn't comment.

Suddenly Sebille seemed to shake off her terror. She stuck her hand out. "I'm Rosalee Reportage. I've come all the way from the Big City to speak to people in this quaint small town. I wonder if you'd be willing to answer some questions for me."

Grym made a choking sound. "Rosalee Reportage?"

I shrugged. "It sounded French. We thought it would seem Big-City-ish."

He shook his head.

"Sure, honey. But you have to order something if you want to stay."

"Oh, oh," I murmured. I glanced at Grym. "Should we abort?"

"Let's just see how she handles it."

"Okay, then I'll have coffee," Sebille said.

The woman poured a cup of black liquid and placed it in front of Sebille. "Cream? Sugar?"

Sebille nodded, opening her notebook and poising her pencil over it. "The title of my story is *The Heart of the Small Town*. Can you tell me in your words what you consider to be Mayberry's heart?"

The waitress settled a creamer and a small container of white granules next to Sebille's cup. "The heart of Mayberry..." she repeated thoughtfully. "Why, I'd guess it's the people."

"Don't be daft, Daisy," an old man called out from a stool down the counter. He turned to look Sebille in the eye. "It's the businesses. Places like this and the Pharmacy down the way. The gas station just outside of town. Even the Sheriff's Office. Those are the heart of the town."

Sebille scribbled as quickly as she could.

"Aren't you gonna drink your coffee?" Daisy asked, narrowing her gaze slightly at the sprite.

Sebille acted like she'd forgotten. "Oh, of course." She gave a little laugh and dumped a bunch of cream into it, followed by several spoons full of sugar. The waitress grimaced at the amount of sugar. Sebille proceeded to stir it as she looked toward a nearby table, where two men sat drinking coffee and reading the paper. "What do you gentlemen think?"

Their heads came up and Sebille spun on her stool, pencil poised over the notebook.

"She's getting the hang of this," Grym said, grinning.

I harrumphed.

The older man pulled a tidy, gray Fedora off his balding head and looked contemplative. Reaching up to scratch his bald spot, he shrugged. "Money's the heart of any community, isn't it?"

The man with him was younger by probably thirty years. Like his companion, he wore a suit and he had his dark hair slicked neatly back. He shook his head, giving the older man a disgusted look. "That's not even close, Frank. Love is everything. Love and affection are the heart of any community."

"Pshaw!" said the man down the counter from Sebille. "Love, schmuve. I say it's the businesses. And that means money's important too."

"Respect!" yelled a woman from a back booth. She wore a tidy cap over her smoothly styled light-colored hair and had short gloves on the hands that clutched a small patent-leather purse. The remains of her lunch sat on a plate in front of her, looking like it had barely been touched. "A community's nothing without respect."

"Miss," said an insistent voice behind Sebille. "You have to drink that coffee."

Sebille looked from one to the other of the people in the restaurant, her lips twitching into a smile as the argument grew heated. The two men at the table stood up, and *Love* strode angrily to the man at the counter, finger stabbing the air as he screamed his arguments into the room.

Money had left his fedora behind and gone to try

to get in between the other two men. He was roughly shoved for his troubles.

Meanwhile, *Respect* had abandoned her uneaten lunch and was stomping toward the battle, a dark gleam in her heated gaze.

"Oh, oh," I said to Grym. "This has taken a turn."

Abort, abort, abort! Yelled a voice in my ear.

On the tiny screen I was holding, the waitress had grabbed Sebille and was trying to pour the coffee down her throat, dodging the flailing note-book and the jabbing pencil.

We started to run. If Sebille accidentally stabbed the waitress in the throat, there'd be a full-on manhunt for her within minutes.

A breeze blew hair from my face as someone passed us going fast.

Really fast.

Hobs fast.

The door slammed open and then closed, the bell jangling from the wild treatment.

A shrill whistle filled the air.

Hobs was inside, standing in front of the door. He wore a cowboy hat on his head and a leather vest covering his tiny chest.

He was chewing on a long piece of grass as Otis had been and held something fat and bug-eyed in his hand.

Slimy?

I started forward in a panic. Grym grabbed my

arm, stopping me. "Let's give this a minute to play out."

We retreated to the alley and watched as Hobs lifted a long-fingered hand and tipped the cowboy hat back. "Howdy, folks," he said in his high-pitched voice. "Me and my pardner are lookin' to wet our whistles."

Sebille extracted herself from the waitress's suddenly nerveless grip and stumbled away, tugging her ugly dress straight.

Hobs tipped his hat. "Hello, Miss."

Sebille's brows spiked upward. "Hey, Tex."

Hobs placed Slimy on the table and *People* the waitress, made a horrified little sound. "You can't put that frog on the table."

Slimy hopped forward and I finally got a good look at him. I gasped. "Is he wearing a cowboy hat?"

Grym snorted. "This is *better* than the circus."

"That's no frog, Miss," Hobs said very carefully, nodding his head as he spoke. "This here's Dark Bart the Bandito. He's a gunslinger. We don't want no trouble, but we're prepared to shoot this place up if'n you don't answer one question for us."

The woman had started nodding along with Hobs. Around her, *Love*, *Money*, *Business* and *Respect* had all begun nodding too. Their eyes glazed over and their mouths started to droop.

"Yes? What question?" asked *People*.

"Ribbit?" Dark Bart belched, his little six-shooters quivering.

Sebille looked at the camera and lifted her brows, clearly asking us if Hobs was really using chicken hypnotization against the people in the diner.

"Yeah," I murmured. "I think he is."

"Ask your question," *Love* droned out as drool slid from his lips onto his shiny shoes.

"What is the Heart of Mayberry?" Hobs asked in a monotone voice.

They all stood there for a long moment, heads bobbing rhythmically and lips shiny with drool. And then, as if spurred by the hand of an invisible puppet master, they all said in perfect unity: "*LoveMoney-BusinessPeopleRespect.*"

"Okay, they all just repeated what they'd already said," I complained. "I always knew hypnosis was hooey."

Grym expelled a sigh.

"It's a bust. Bring it in, people," I said into the little microphone on the cell.

"Ribbit!" said Dark Bart, his squishy little form taut with anger.

Hobs yanked what looked like a toy gun from the holster at his narrow hips. "You've gone and done it now. You've angered Dark Bart. You give us no choice but to shoot up the joint."

"Excuse me, please, sir?" A small voice said.

Hobs turned to find a small, freckled-faced boy entering the diner. It was Opie, the Sheriff's son.

Hobbs spun around and pointed the gun at the newcomer, before quickly jerking it back. "Oh, hello."

Opie studied him from under a thick fringe of bangs. "Isn't it 'lectricity?"

Hobs frowned, "Lectricity?"

Opie nodded, looking ever so serious. "That's what Pa says. 'Lectricity makes the world go round. I reckon that would be the heart o' anything. Ain't that right?"

Hobbs opened his mouth to reply and...the world erupted into noise and pain.

I dropped the phone to cover my ears, doubling over into a ball as small as I could go, given my inherent lack of bendiness. Beside me, Grym shoved to his feet and started to run, his voice a weak murmur against the air-raid-siren blaring through the artifact.

I forced myself to reach for the phone and stand, stumbling after Grym with my hands pressed to my ears.

He'd disappeared from sight by the time I rounded the corner at the end of the alley. I figured he'd gone to help Sebille and Hobs in the diner, so I started off in that direction.

I never made it to the diner.

An enormous, rectangular car slammed to a stop

on the street next to me, and a dark-haired man with a black, hostile gaze threw the door open and jumped on me, riding me to the concrete in a decidedly hostile takedown maneuver.

Sebille's phone flew from my hand and clattered away, falling toward the gutter.

"I finally got you, ya varmint!" the man exclaimed, yanking my arms behind my back and cuffing them together. "Maybe you can help us find the rest of the trouble-makers." He yanked me up by my arms, wrenching them painfully enough that I cried out, and all but threw me into the wide backseat of the big police car.

I rolled painfully to my side and shoved myself to a seated position as the Sheriff of Mayberry's car eased away from the curb. "What am I under arrest for?" I asked, my voice embarrassingly whiney.

The dark-eyed man turned in his seat, the signature sweep of his dark hair still perfect despite his overly-rough handling of yours truly. He gave me a mean smile, his homely face darkening with TV effect as he did. "You're under arrest for whatever I say you are," said Sheriff Andrew. "And we're taking you where nobody else is gonna find you. So you'd better cooperate, or you're gonna have a very unhappy ending."

"Boy," I said in the face of all that oily evil. "You're mean. I feel sorry for Opie having you for a dad."

He gave me a villainous laugh and turned back around, leaving me to my thoughts and despair.

Way to go, Naida, I grumbled to myself. *You really set him straight with that one.*

Sigh...

15

TELEVISION LIES SO HARD

I huddled in the dank, dark corner and looked around, my nose twitching under the dual assault of mold and dust.

My wrists were raw from the pair of iron cuffs that were bolted into the concrete wall. I jerked on them and frowned, wishing for the comfy TV jail cell with the key within easy reach.

Television lied so hard.

Sheriff Andrew wasn't kind and harmless. Not even close to the friendly country bumpkin television portrayed him as. If only bumbling Deputy Fiff were around. I could probably talk him into letting me go. He wasn't any nicer than the Sheriff, but he was much dumber.

The only door in the building opened with a creak that made me jump. Sunlight speared across the space, highlighting a mildewed dirt floor with lots of suspicious little black pellets that made my skin crawl.

The hulking form of the Sheriff truncated the sunlight, casting an elongated shadow across the floor. He didn't speak for a long moment, making it impossible to judge his mood. His expression was hidden in shadow. But his hands were fisted at his sides, and the set of his shoulders was rigid.

I glared back at him, clinging to defiance like dog spit clings to paint. "My friends are going to find me and you'll be sorry."

I doubted that was true since even I had no idea where I was. But I was proud that my voice didn't quiver on the empty threat.

He continued to stare mutely in my direction.

I jerked the cuffs again and tried to climb to my feet, feeling at a disadvantage sitting there. It was no use. The cuffs were bolted too low. Even if I managed to get to my feet, I'd be hunched over with my butt in the air.

Not exactly an intimidating posture.

Unless he was scared over how wide my butt was.

The sheriff came into the room, his face moving from the shadows. I was surprised by his pleasant, harmless expression.

It was his lying television face.

"Now, now. There's no call to get hostile. I just

wanted ta ask y'all a couple of questions. There's no harm in that, is there?"

I jerked the cuffs again. "There's definite harm in these cuffs. Take them off, and I'll answer your questions."

He laughed, shoving his hands into the pockets of his pale uniform pants. "Now that ain't gonna happen." He cocked his head. "Why don't you tell me what y'all are up to?"

I jerked the cuffs again, glaring at him.

"Now, Miss, you're just gonna bruise yourself all up. Why don't you just tell me what I want to know and we can go have some of Aint Bee's fried chicken and mashed potatoes?" He gave me the goofy TV smile. "Y'all'd like that, wouldn't ya?"

"I'd love some chicken and potatoes. I'd even love some pie. But not at the expense of all my friends."

He expelled air on a sigh, shaking his head. But he was still smiling. Unfortunately, the smile didn't reach his black eyes. "We're gonna find out what y'all are up to and we're gonna stop ya anyway we can. You'd best tell me now, and maybe we'll spare yore friends."

"How about this, instead? You let me and my friends go home. Problem solved."

He looked down at his dusty boots. "You're tryin' my patience now, gal."

I shrugged. "I'm sorry about that. But that's the only deal I'll take."

"Well, then I guess you leave me no choice." He rubbed his hand over his chin.

The ground beneath me rumbled. Dust sifted down from the rough clay ceiling above my head. The light beyond the door dimmed, and dark clouds filled the once-blue sky. "What are you doing?" I asked, fear tightening my chest.

"What you're forcin' me ta do." He headed for the door and stopped, looking back. "It's a darn shame too. I grown fond of the people in this little town. It's a shame ta have ta lose 'em all. And in so violent a way too." He shook his head and sighed again. Then he lifted a hand in a wave. "Bye now!"

The door slammed hard enough to dislodge something from a dark corner. I yelped in surprise as the hard, white orb rolled into view, bumping against my foot. And I screamed again as I realized what it was.

Black holes in the bleached skull stared accusingly out at me. I scrambled backward as best I could when a long, humanoid bone rolled out to join the skull, smashing myself against the damp, slimy concrete.

Outside my prison, thunder boomed hard and long, shaking the shed and pulling all the light from the room. The slivers of sky I could see through the small cracks of my prison showed darkness where moments earlier it had been bright daylight. Jagged spears of lightning sheared through the dark, illuminating the shed in bright bolts of white energy that left behind the sound of crashing and screaming in the distance.

My prison shook more with every boom above my head. Ozone stung my nostrils. Without warning, energy whistled through the air and slammed into the little building, exploding the wall across from me and fracturing my world into ear-splitting, deadly chunks of misery.

I woke up sometime later, a heavy weight against my chest. I realized I'd been fighting to breathe for a while, dreaming of being underwater and struggling not to drown.

I came awake with a gasp and a strangled scream.

Inhaling more dust than air, I choked, coughing and wheezing to pull breath into lungs that felt weighed down by a million pounds and clogged with filth.

Forcing myself to calm, I lay there a moment, listening to the world beyond my broken prison. The sky was visible above me. One chunk of the wall where the door was had collapsed. It was dark both outside and inside the moldy hut.

There was silence in the distance and I wondered if everyone was gone. Surely Andrew hadn't followed through on his threat to kill everyone.

What would be the point in that?

I coughed and cried out in pain. Something was digging into my chest...something heavy and sharp.

I tried to lift my hands to examine the problem and found they wouldn't move. I was trapped under heavy concrete debris.

Parakeet pullups! No wonder I couldn't breathe.

Panic swirled through me, making it even harder to breathe as my heart pounded in my ears.

Nobody knew where I was. How were they going to find me?

Small, panicked noises escaped my throat and silvery stars burst in front of my eyes.

I was trapped! Forgotten! Lost!

When I realized that I was in danger of hyper-ventilating, I forced my breathing to slow. After a moment, pushing the panic aside, I was able to form thoughts again. I could try to use my keeper magics. Worst case my efforts would just make a lot of noise. But if that happened, maybe it would help my friends locate where I was. *Of course*, my treacherous brain told me, *it could just call Sheriff Andrew back to finish me off.* I shoved that thought away. I had to do something. And best case was that I'd call something useful to me. There had to be some artifacts in Mayberry, didn't there? I mean, I'd brought that dang, useless pie-making thing with me, hadn't I?

I wriggled my fingers free of debris and, with a supreme force of will, managed to wring some of my magic from its core, dragging it slowly through my limbs toward my waiting fingers. It was like shoving sludge through a straw. I wondered if being in the anti-magic artifact world was somehow changing my magic. Turning it thick and slow.

The thought was daunting and it made me even more determined to get out of there.

Silvery energy burned the tips of my fingers, the occasional spark flaring into the darkness. I felt better just seeing it there, knowing I had something I could use to help myself.

It wasn't much. But it was more than I'd had a moment earlier.

Closing my eyes, I concentrated on the thick stream of waiting energy. With a thought toward calling artifacts to me, I let it go, my eyes snapping open as the magic slithered slowly away from my fingers like flat, silver snakes, undulating away into the dark.

I watched the magic slide through the open areas and cracks and writhe away through the night. As soon as the energy was out of sight, panic eased back to claim me.

Nothing had happened. No screaming sirens

filled the night. I hadn't sent up a magical beacon that my friends could follow.

If my energy didn't bring anything back, I was in trouble.

Ice slid along my spine and spread through me. A beat later, I realized I was shivering, my teeth clanking together from the cold.

I closed my eyes and tried to pull more energy forward, hoping it would make me warm.

But nothing came. The piddly little worms of magic had been everything I had.

And they'd brought nothing back.

Fighting despair and quaking with the cold, I closed my eyes and tried not to give in to the raging fear climbing through my chest.

Something clattered to the rock covering my chest.

My eyes snapped open.

The pig-pimpled, never-ending pie plate sat a few inches from my nose, a sweet, creamy scent mingling with the dust and mold.

I sneezed and the plate shifted off the debris, toppling to the rock below. With a soft, cracking sound, it broke, and the slimy sweetness of chocolate cream oozed into the cracks.

A beat later, I felt it hit my arm and dribble over my skin.

"Awesome-sauce," I muttered, tears burning my eyes.

I lay there a moment longer, giving in to the tears. I became gradually aware of something poking into my side and shifted away from it.

My arm slid easily along the rock covering it. My eyes went wide. I shifted again, rubbing the slimy pie filling over the rock and using the lubrication it gave to move my arm until I managed to free it from the rocky prison.

With hope soaring in my heart, I dug for another glob of pie filling and lubricated my other arm with it, eventually working it free with the help of the sweet lubricant.

But that was as far as a slice of pie could take me. My thighs were still firmly pinned.

The air shifted on a sigh, and I winced as a rectangular object flew toward my face.

I yelped, my hands snapping up to catch it before it connected. Squinting through the dark at the object, I tried to figure out what it was. The front was dominated by two big dials, and there was something attached to the back, like a fuzzy snake.

I ran my fingers over the snake and realized it was a cord. I was holding an old-fashioned radio. A lot of good it would do me. Unless it ran on batteries.

Or magic.

As my fingers found the plug on the end of a badly frayed cord, the dials lit up and a rusty song filled the air. "What the?"

I settled the radio onto the rocks and turned the

dial, looking for something besides old country songs.

Another object sighed through the air and clattered to the ground next to me, sending chips of rock and a puff of dust into the air.

I sneezed again, my hand spasming on the dial, and an old-timey news guy's voice suddenly replaced the music.

"Sheriff Andrew has instructed everyone to remain calm. The tornados have moved on and he and Deputy Fiff are organizing rescue squads as I give you this report. If you are lost or trapped, the Sheriff wanted me to tell you that he *will* find you." The voice on the radio deepened and turned louder, sounding as if he'd pressed his lips closer to the microphone. "That is a promise." I shuddered as I realized he was talking to me. Or maybe to my friends.

The Sheriff was creating search parties all right. But they weren't to rescue people from the chaos the artifact had created. They were to find and extinguish the small rebellion Dugan and his gang had begun.

I needed to get out of there and warn them.

It didn't matter that they might hear the radio announcement too. I doubted they'd recognize the significance of it.

I turned to see what had flown into my prison after the radio. The soft glow of the radio's dials illuminated something long and skinny, wider on one end. By moving the radio to illuminate it better, I was able to finally identify the object as a pitchfork.

My heart palpitated a few times as I realized how easily the thing could have skewered me. But it hadn't, I told myself. And it could be very useful.

Shoving the radio to the side, I strained against the rocks piled over my hips and legs and reached for the pitchfork.

My fingers couldn't quite touch the handle. If I risked pulling all my limbs out of their sockets, I could just about get my fingertips on the smooth surface. I pressed with my fingers, sweating from the effort, and the fork moved a fraction of an inch closer.

I collapsed back, gasping. It was still too far away to grab.

I strained again and managed another quarter of an inch. It wasn't enough to grab the fork, but it was enough to allow me to pull it closer.

Another five minutes of struggling and I wrapped my fingers around the heavy implement.

I held it above me, looking up at it, and realized it was long and really heavy. Too heavy from my half-buried position to get much leverage.

But I didn't have any choice. I had to try. So I worked my hands along the handle until they grasped the wide metal head and then flipped it over, settling the tips underneath the biggest rock holding me in place.

Then I began the nearly impossible process of trying to burrow the prongs underneath the thick slab of concrete.

16

MAKEUP!

Whether an hour or several hours later, it really didn't matter because, however long it took, it just about destroyed me. I shoved at the last rock holding me down with shaking arms and lay back, panting. My arms quivered with weariness. My head was pounding, probably more from dehydration than anything else, and my hands were bleeding so badly the pitchfork had slipped from my grip and clattered to the ground on my final effort.

I needed to move. But all I wanted to do was lie there, praying for a miracle. If I closed my eyes and knocked my heels together three times, would I wake up at Croakies?

The thought brought tears burning in my eyes. I missed home.

I missed my friends.

I missed comfort and tea and...brownies.

Yeah, that last part might have been inspired by the residual scent of the pie-making plate. I glanced toward the broken remnants, the first soft rays of dawn bathing the spot in a jagged, pale light and showing two equal plate halves, holding two perfect triangles of pie.

I grinned. Well, at least something had gone right. I reached over and grabbed the first succulent slice of lemon cream pie and started eating. By the time I'd finished both slices, I had the energy to climb to my feet. I grabbed the plate pieces and shoved them together, trapping the 2 fresh slices in the middle, and slipped it inside my shirt for later.

I grimaced as cool peach filling slid from the sides. I'd be a sticky mess. But at least I wouldn't be hungry.

I grabbed the pitchfork and carefully picked my way through the broken concrete and clay debris that was all that was left of my prison. As I stepped through the fractured wall, the sun broke over a distant line of trees, bathing me in a pale gray light.

I inhaled deeply, relishing the first dust and mold-free breath I'd taken since the Sheriff had imprisoned me there, and turned toward a low line of buildings in the distance. It didn't look like Mayberry. But that might be a good thing. I'd locate shelter, get my bearings, and find a way to notify my friends where I was.

Feeling much better for having a plan, I set off toward the town on the horizon.

Only a few minutes had passed before the air sighed and split an inch from my nose, making me jump back with a yelp. A slender column of painted wood smacked the nearest tree with a "thwuck".

I instinctively ducked, my gaze going to the tree and widening. "Holy fish fingers!" An arrow quivered there, embedded in the dense bark, and I realized it had been meant for me.

Another arrow soughed through the air and hit the dirt inches from my feet. I jumped straight up in the air with a yelp and scurried over to the skewered tree, diving behind it for protection.

Two more arrows hit the ground around the tree. I clutched my pitchfork in sweaty palms, feeling as if I'd entered a gun battle clutching a butter knife.

The ground thundered beneath my knees. With a pounding pulse, I glanced up to the sky, expecting more bad news to be roiling there. But the sky was still light, with wispy layers of white clouds.

Realizing the current trouble was situated much lower, I peered cautiously around the tree. Three horses galloped my way, dust flaring around their hooves. Perched easily on their bare backs, three shirtless, dark-haired riders sent feral screams into the dawn sky. The two on the outside carried long spears above their heads, their screams warbling aggressively in their throats. The rider in the middle nocked an arrow on the fly, piercing the tree mere inches from my face.

I slammed backward. "Indians? Really?" My achy breaky heart thundered in my chest. I didn't want to be killed and scalped by men wearing too little cloth and too much war paint. I liked my hair right where it was, thank you. And I preferred my men fully clothed.

Well...mostly.

I scanned the area, looking for an escape route and seeing nothing.

I took stock of my defensive options. I had two. I could either distract them with pie or try to poke them with my pitchfork.

I was pretty sure they'd be much better with their spears than I was with my pitchfork. And while I poked at them, the guy with the arrows would put more holes in me than my favorite tea infuser.

Sometimes my life sucked a bushel of lemons.

The three horses slammed to a stop not far from the tree. I gripped the fork, taking a deep breath for courage. A beat later, I jumped from behind the tree, crouching with my weapon in front of me and trying to look fierce.

The three men stood straight and tall, their black eyes hostile in their broad faces. One of them flared wide nostrils and frowned. "Where's your pretty dress? The parasol? You're a mess."

I blinked. "Huh?" Way to dazzle Naida.

The one with the bow sighed with irritation. "Makeup!" he shouted.

The horizon moved and a young woman wearing jeans and a tidy checkered shirt stepped out from behind it. I realized I'd been looking at a backdrop. She placed hands on hips. "What is it now, Fonzie?"

Fonzie?

The bow guy flung a hand in my direction. "Why isn't the damsel in distress in costume? She looks like something from a deserted island episode. I'm not taking *that* prisoner. She's a mess. And she smells like a prisoner of war movie."

The girl glowered at me. "You were supposed to get into costume. I'm not your mother. I'm not dressing you. Now get your butt over to makeup and see if they can fix you up. Maybe visit the *Contagion* set and have them give you one of those disinfecting showers. I'm pretty sure you need more than just soap and water."

I scowled back at her, my dignity in tatters around me, and then realized she'd given me the perfect out. Biting back an instinctive defense of my condition, I lowered my head and stumbled in the direction she'd pointed, leaving them all arguing unhappily behind me.

The line of buildings I'd seen in the distance were definitely not Mayberry. It reminded me of the western town I'd seen in Behind the Scenes.

I stopped in the middle of the dusty street and

stared at the buildings. They were built of rough wood and their windows were sans glass. The building in the center, the *Okay Saloon*, had a covered wooden porch containing a rustic pair of rocking chairs and a lot of mud. Two people rocked slowly in the chairs, giving me slanty-eyed looks filled with disgust. The woman was dressed in a risqué bustier that showed more than it hid and a ruffled black skirt that frothed around her slender calves, just over a pair of leather lace-up boots. Her long legs were crossed and the uppermost boot bounced on the air as she scowled in my direction. "You look like something the Native Americans dragged in."

The person in the other rocker, a long, lean man wearing a white cowboy hat he'd pushed back on his head, laughed. He gave me a crooked smile, his teeth perfectly white and straight around the piece of hay he was chewing. "Honey, you're gonna give Mabel a run for her money."

I frowned. "Mabel?"

The swinging doors of the saloon slammed open, and a bony blonde stood there, her small face mutinous. "Finally! I was told you'd be here an hour ago." Her pale eyes flashed with rage. "And look at you. What have you been doing?" She narrowed her gaze. "Did they send me the heroine for the prisoner of war episode instead?"

I opened my mouth to respond but never got the

chance. Mable shoved a swinging door open and screamed back the way she'd come. "Hey! Lance, did you grab the wrong list of acters again?"

A disembodied male voice emerged from the darkened interior, the response more swears than actual words. Suffice it to say it didn't bear repeating.

Mable rolled her eyes like she'd been doing it all her life. Her eye muscles must have been spectacular. I was wondering if she'd be willing to do a roll-off against the sprite, and had opened my mouth to ask her as she stomped out to the street and grabbed my arm, dragging me toward the building. "Come on. We only have a few minutes to get you ready. Those Indians are charging by the hour, and they're costing us a fortune."

I barely had time to take in the interior of the Saloon as she dragged me past wooden tables filled with men dressed in Western gear, complete with long-barreled guns shoved into leather holsters strapped around muscular thighs. Several more women dressed like the one in the rocker outside lounged among the men, drinking something frothy from heavy glasses.

Saloon girls.

I grinned. I'd never met a saloon girl before.

Mable shoved me through a door, and I found myself standing in a plain room with a narrow bed and a curtained-off area that had a makeshift shower. "Strip and clean up. There's soap and stuff in that basket. If you're not back out here in five minutes, I'm coming in after you."

She tugged the curtain closed and I hurried to strip. But only because, at that point, I would have killed to be clean. I wasn't afraid that the scrawny tyrant would yank me naked from the shower.

No. I. Was. Not.

The pie plate slipped down my belly when I removed my shirt and I grabbed it before it shattered on the ground. Looking around, I found a spot behind the basket to hide it, figuring I could come back to get it once I was dressed again.

I took the fastest shower I've ever taken, the water only warm but still feeling wonderful against my griminess. I watched as a semi-solid clump of pie filling globbed off me onto the rough wood floor and got caught in the drain. I smiled. Let them try to figure out what that was when they went to clean it later.

Light, rapid footsteps on the wood planks beyond the curtains warned me just as I tugged a towel around my body. I stepped through as Mable lifted a bony hand to open the curtains.

She looked at me, seemingly annoyed that she hadn't gotten to roust me and said, "Hmph."

I followed her to the narrow bed and she tugged a lacy white concoction from the top, handing it to me. I held it up with one hand, the other hand busy clutching the towel around my dripping nakedness. "What's this?"

Mable frowned. "Are you serious? They haven't taught you about all the parts of your costume?"

I shook my head, not having to fake my cluelessness.

Mable repeated one or two of Lance's creative swears and grabbed it back from me. "Dry off. I guess I'm going to have to dress you like a baby."

A half-hour later, feeling bruised and traumatized from being threatened and bludgeoned into a light-gray cotton dress with lace along its way-too-low neckline and around its short, puffy sleeves, I stumbled through the door back into the saloon.

A chorus of wolf-whistles filled the room at my arrival.

The three Indians who'd tried to skewer me with arrows and spears were standing at the bar drinking firewater. They turned and gave me an appreciative look. The one with the bow and arrows waggled his brows.

I blushed. I'd have felt good about the positive attention, except I was pretty sure it was just because my boobs were all but hanging out of the stupid dress. I tugged on the neckline again, gaining nothing for my efforts except another slap on the hand by Mable.

"You clean up pretty well," said a feminine voice I

recognized. I turned to find the woman from the rocking chair sauntering in my direction. She reached out and tugged on a shiny curl Mable had used her magical powers to create in my long, brown hair. I had to admit, the woman had a way with recalcitrant, bossy brown hair. "I would have never believed *that* was under all the filth," said rocker lady.

I stared at her, recognizing a back-handed compliment when I heard one.

Go me.

She smiled, glancing toward Mable. "I'll get her to her mark and make sure she's got her lines down."

Mabel's glower softened. "That would be very helpful, Donia. Thank you."

Donia hooked her arm through mine and sashayed toward the door as if her hips were attached to a rowing machine. Her firm flesh bounced against mine as we reached the door, and I would have stumbled sideways from the contact if she hadn't been clinging to my arm.

Grinning widely, she released me and sashayed gracefully through the door. I followed her through, feeling like an ungainly oaf next to her supple beauty.

The sun drilled into my eyes as I stepped outside. I squinched them to slits, reaching up to tug on my neckline again as sunlight threatened to bake the pasty white flesh there. Expecting Donia to lead me back to the copse of trees where I'd been set upon by the painted-pony-riding natives, I was surprised when she tugged me down the street. Glancing frantically around, I tried to come up with an excuse to escape.

I didn't get the chance. Donia yanked me sideways, into the shade of the faux buildings. "Come on."

I stumbled over my shoes and fell into her wake, trying to yank my arm from her iron grip. "Where are we going?" I was pretty sure she wasn't interested in helping me with my lines. But I wasn't getting a good vibe about what she *did* want to do with me. "Are you friends with Sheriff Andrew?"

Donia tugged me into a haberdashery and yanked the door closed behind us. I blinked at the grass and dirt under my feet, spinning back to look at the front of the room.

Nothing but unpainted wood.

It was just a set, consisting only of a front façade and nothing else. Donia reached for me again. I yanked my arm away. "Whoa, girl. I'm not moving again until you tell me where we're going."

She expelled a frustrated breath. "I'm trying to help."

"Okay. Help how?"

"You don't belong here. I happen to know that somebody's looking for you the next show over."

Alarm made my chest tighten. "You *do* work with Andrew."

She snorted. "Not hardly. If it was up to me, we would have welded that guy into his big ugly car a long time ago." She frowned. "I'm friends with a certain old Irish guy. We got here about the same time."

The tightness in my chest eased. "You know Dugan?"

She nodded. "When you disappeared, they told me to keep an eye out for you."

I grabbed her hand, "Are they okay? My friends?"

Donia sighed. "I think so. I only talked to Dugan for a minute. We're under careful watch. The only place that's safe is Behind the Scenes."

"Like here?" I asked, waving a hand around the open lot.

"No. This is just a backlot. They can still see us here. We can't stay. We need to go back out there. I just wanted to warn you that things are heating up. The best you can do is pretend you're where you're supposed to be. And don't eat anything."

I shook my head. "We need to get out of here. I have no idea how much time has passed back home. I've got responsibilities, people counting on me." What I left unspoken was my debilitating fear of getting stuck in that horrible place. I figured that was a given.

Donia leaned closer, her gaze on mine. "We're working on that. We've been working on it for years. We could use your help. But let me make one thing very clear. We won't allow you to screw things up. If you get in our way, we'll treat you just like we treat *them*. Do I make myself clear?"

By the way she said *them*, I figured she wasn't talking about her friends.

It was a threat.

Gulp.

"Look, I'm not going to get in the way, but I need to find my friends. I need to know they're okay."

Donia shook her head, clearly disgusted with me. "This is bigger than just you and your friends. There are a lot of people here who want to get back to their families and friends. I need to know if you're with us or not." The clear implication was that, if I wasn't "with" Donia in the way she wanted me to be, then I was against her.

I didn't want to be against her. She and I had the same goals. And I didn't need any more enemies. So, I nodded. "I'm with you. What do you want me to do?"

She grabbed the door we'd come through. "You're about to get kidnapped by Indians. But don't worry," she said as she shoved me through the door ahead of her. "The cowboys will rescue you. I just hope it happens before you lose all that pretty brown hair."

I didn't miss the implied threat. Icy fingers slid down my spine. Donia was crazy. I didn't need friends like that. I already had enemies like that.

But, I needed to play along, bide my time. And look for a way to get back to Mayberry to find my friends.

As I stumbled back toward the tree I'd hidden behind before, I couldn't help noticing the irony. When had Mayberry become my happy zone?

17

I'M NEVER WATCHING TV AGAIN!

I crouched in the grubby street, my hair hanging in my face and dust thickening the air as ponies and horses cavorted around me in a terrifying dance, the stench of what I hoped was faux gunpowder making my nose itch.

My hands were tied behind my back, the rough rope rubbing painfully against my skin, and a nasty tasting cloth was jammed into my mouth. I was pretty sure it was somebody's sock. From the smell and taste, I was convinced it hadn't been clean when it was jammed between my lips.

I scrambled away with a yelp as a painted pony sidestepped toward me, its small neat hooves leaving imprints in the dirt where I'd been. Not for the first time, I wondered if Donia had actually decided I was against the group of rebels and was trying to take me out after all.

The sun beat down on my head, turning the skin on my pale, pale bosom pink. *Toasted tarantulas*! I was going to be burned to a crisp even if I managed to survive my faux captivity.

A bullet kicked up dirt three inches from my foot and I screamed behind the dirty sock, scrambling toward a nearby tree as fast as my bound feet and hands would allow.

Dramatic music swelled around me, making my pulse spike as it gave the impression something dire was coming. *Dum, der, dum, dum, dadadadadum!*

I shook uncontrollably, knowing I'd never look at a soundtrack the same way again.

Sighing with relief, I managed to find a ribbon of shade in the scalding street. The music turned insistent, the notes pounding with tension. I held my breath and looked around, gaze widening with fear.

A thick bank of gray clouds skimmed by overhead, momentarily crowding out the sun as a moisture-filled breeze skimmed past.

Was the artifact going to throw another tantrum? And, if it did, would I survive? I was trapped out there in the open. Bound and helpless against anything it decided to fling my way.

I struggled against the ropes, ignoring pain from my tearing flesh as I fought to get myself free.

Dum, der dum, dum, dadadadaDUM!

Two figures appeared out of the dust.

The bass warning in the music throbbed in the center of my chest, followed by the shrill slash of string instruments that scraped across my already taut nerves. I stilled, feeling the tension change around me.

The Indians lifted their spears and shrieked, the sound a call to battle in the face of new danger.

The cowboys took protected locations, their guns falling silent as the soundtrack formed an emotional path for the newly-arrived gunmen to follow.

I swallowed hard, forgetting the ropes abrading the flesh of my wrists and ankles, as the two new players stopped at the end of the street.

The sight struck me breathless. I sucked back, pressing against the tree in renewed terror. I shoved at the stinky gag with my tongue, frantic to get my mouth clear so I could shout a warning.

The nasty cloth stuck to my tongue, making me retch.

A wiry figure stood in the distance, hat set low on his round head. His features were hidden, his stance taut. The gun in his hands was huge, glinting in a flash of sunlight as the clouds moved on past. The cowboy wore two more guns in holsters slung low on his hips. He stood with legs braced, long-fingered hands wrapped confidently around the rifle.

As I watched, he racked a shell into the chamber of the big gun and spit something nasty into the dirt.

"You're not takin' the girl," he called out. "Best you just take yourselves out of my town, or you're gonna be talkin' to the spirits of your ancestors sooner than you were expectin'."

I frowned. Bad dialogue. Really bad.

The gunman's partner was shorter than him and widely made. But his hat sat just as low on his head, his features obscured by the dusty felt. The guns still holstered on his hips told the people watching the stand-off that he didn't think he needed to draw down on the intruders. He was almost cocky in his dismissal of them.

I knew better. If push came to shove. He was gonna die. And there was nothing I could do about it. I tried to cough the rag from between my lips. It stayed glued to my tongue. Refusing to be dislodged.

In desperation, I attempted to bend closer to my knees, hoping I could trap the cloth between them and tug.

But I'm not bendy. And I'd never regretted it more than at that moment.

The tension between the two factions in the street broke suddenly as one of the Indians jumped down from his painted pony and, with a bloodcurdling scream, launched his spear toward the taller cowboy.

The street went silent as the deadly weapon sliced toward its target.

The cowboy squeezed the trigger in answer, the sound exploding through the waiting street.

I wanted to close my eyes, but they wouldn't close. I was trapped in the agony of expectation, certain I was going to watch the cowboy die.

Three things happened at once.

One, the slug found the Indian with the bow and arrow and threw him backward off the pony. He hit the dirty street with a pain-filled, "Umph!" and went still.

Two, the music shrieked in a crescendo of shared agony.

And three, the spear slammed into its target.

The point drove deep, the shaft quivering violently as it met the resistance of an unyielding surface, and flew back into the air again smacking the cowboy right between the eyes.

His oversized hat flew backward, spinning across the dusty street.

All around me, gasps sounded beneath the softly throbbing music. We all stared at the spear lying in the street, and the cowboy rubbing his bleeding nose.

We waited.

I fought to spit out the rag.

And the shorter cowboy swallowed hard, looking up at his pardner.

Then the taller cowboy smiled, grabbing the

shaft of the spear off the ground and screaming, "Again!"

The tension burst, the music swelled in happy tones, and the Indians whirled their ponies around and headed out of town, defeated.

The shorter cowboy hopped a few times with joy and said, "Ribbit!"

I sagged back against the tree. Spent. I'd thought for sure I'd lost them both that time.

"Cut!" Someone yelled. "That's a wrap."

A moment later, hard hands tugged at my ropes. I felt warm metal sliding between my palms. "Stay still, Naida."

My eyes shot open and I looked up into Grym's worried face. He forced a smile. "We thought we'd never find you."

I closed my eyes, fighting tears. I'd thought they'd never find me too.

Grym helped me stand and held onto my arm as the blood rushed back into my feet.

"I'm never watching TV again," I told him.

To my surprise, Grym pulled me into his arms and held on tight. "You really scared us."

"Sorry. I didn't mean to. Sheriff Andrew grabbed me." I frowned. "He said he'd blown up Mayberry. Is that why you're all here?"

He shook his head. "He was just playing mind games with you. Unfortunately, Mayberry's fine." He jerked his head toward the woman standing across the street. "She told us you were here."

Donia's eyes flashed with some emotion I couldn't read. It sure looked like hostility, but I had no idea why. She slowly inclined her head and then turned to re-enter the saloon without a word.

"Come on, the group's waiting for us."

I didn't get a chance to move before a bony, big-eared projectile slammed into me, nearly taking me down to the street again. I looked down at the hobgoblin wrapped around me.

"We were so worried, Miss."

I wrapped myself around him, hugging him tightly in return. "I'm okay, Hobs."

He nodded, finally stepping back. He wiped tears from his cheeks. I pointed to his bleeding nose. "Are you all right?"

He grinned. "That was fun."

"Ha!" I said, shaking my head. "Your definition of fun and mine are vastly different."

"Ribbit." I looked down at the dusty frog, grinning. I couldn't help myself. The getup was just so cute. "Hey, Slimy. You make a darn cute...erm... handsome cowboy."

"Ribbit!" He hopped again, turning his back on me. I got the distinct impression he wasn't thrilled with me calling him cute.

Reaching down, I scooped him up, kissing him on the nose.

"Come on," Grym said.

I followed him and Hobs out of town, into the countryside.

It didn't take me long to forget I was glad to see them. It was hot and dry and I was so tired. "How far is it?"

Grym skimmed me a smile. "Not far." He pointed toward the sparkling pond in the distance. "They're waiting for us in the culvert."

"Why?"

Grym didn't respond for a moment. I nudged him with an elbow. "What's up?"

He sighed. "They found us at Behind the Scenes. We had to move."

"We almost didn't escape," Hobs added, earning himself a glare from Grym.

Apparently, there was a plan to keep me in the dark. Did they think I'd blame myself? Or, did they think I'd given them away? Yikes!

"To the culvert?" My voice was decidedly shrill. I immediately shut it down, clearing my throat. But fear slipped cold fingers around my heart and squeezed. The artifact was closing in on us. We needed to make our move and fast.

I hadn't wanted to talk about what I'd figured out when I'd been imprisoned in the moldy hut. But I realized we were running out of time. I turned to

Grym. "I think I have an idea how to shut the artifact down."

"Oh, oh," he said.

I followed his gaze toward the large, boxy car speeding toward us in the distance.

Sheriff Mayberry had found us!

18

GOBSMACKED GRASSHOPPER SNOT!

G rym grabbed my arm and started running, pulling me along behind him. I stumbled over a rock and almost went down, my grip on Mr. Slimy making him croak out his dismay.

I regained my balance and let Grym drag me toward a line of tall evergreens. A nearby tree exploded in a wash of wood splinters and biting needles. The peppery scent of evergreen tar filled my nostrils, and we picked up speed as another bullet slammed into the dirt by my feet.

I yelped, lowering my head and trying to ignore the burning pain in my chest as my body ran out of juice. It had been a tough couple of days. I'd been running on little food or water and not much sleep.

Grym never wavered, his feet unerringly finding the path ahead of us and his strong hand keeping me upright. Hobs easily kept ahead of us. Even unenhanced by magic, his speed was easily three times ours.

As we ducked between trees, zigging and zagging through their dense, prickly branches, the bullets gradually fell away, striking well behind us. I knew it wouldn't last. Andrew and Fiff would eventually catch up. But I had to bite down on a request to stop, wanting only to catch my breath. Grym ran on, his purpose unwavering. And I realized we were no longer heading toward the pond.

I jerked away from him and stood panting, bending at the waist until I could talk. "We're going the wrong way."

Barely breathing hard, Grym shook his head. "We can't lead Andrew to the culvert."

Through my weariness, it took me a beat to realize what he was saying.

We were on our own.

Again.

Gobsmacked grasshopper snot!

The sound of guns firing got me moving again. I took off after Grym, Hobs skimming the ground ahead of us.

Then Hobs dropped from view, only a surprised yelp alerting us as we flew up behind him. By the time we realized what had happened, it was too late to adjust.

Grym's arms splayed wide and he plunged downward. Too close behind him to stop, I yelped as the ground fell away from my feet and then screamed as I dropped into the earth.

We probably plummeted for several seconds, though it felt much longer. I eventually smacked into something smooth and slick, caterwauling like a cat in heat as the smooth surface turned my fall to a fast glide. I was in a semi-vertical tunnel, like an upright coffin that was trying to dump me out.

Stars burst before my gaze as panic raced through me. My chest tightened to the point of pain. I'd never thought too much about whether I was claustrophobic. I realized in that moment that I definitely was.

Suffice it to say, it was a bad time to come to that realization.

Light flared past me as I slid toward the center of the earth. A soft light that was an eerie green color which felt somehow wrong. The illumination seemed to come from the spaces between the rocky layers as if it was seeping from somewhere else.

The temperature of the space increased as we fell. I pictured us plummeting toward the earth's molten center. Then I remembered we weren't on the earth.

Or at least I didn't think we were. I really didn't know where we were.

The abyss? But where was that? Outer space? Inner space?

My brain hurt from trying to figure it out.

A happy shriek made my pulse spike, followed by Hobs' not too surprising, "Again!"

If I wasn't plunging into the earth at a terrifying rate, I might even have smiled at that.

Far below me, I heard Grym's heavy body smacking into the ground and bouncing a couple of times, then his long, drawn-out groan.

The vertical tunnel narrowed further, teasing my newfound claustrophobia to new heights. The enveloping rock brushed against my wider hips and shoulders, slowing my descent.

The tunnel finally opened up into a massive cavern and pooped me out onto the ground beneath. I hit a moss-covered floor that was made of moist clay, which didn't give a lot when I hit. The bright green moss was just enough to transform my impact from bone-breaking to merely painful.

Green! My mind finally registered the return of color. Something had changed.

Maybe we weren't in Kansas anymore.

I lay there a moment, my face buried in cool green froth, and groaned out my pain. My whole body hurt.

"You okay?" a deep voice asked.

I rolled over and groaned again, just in case he'd missed it the first time. "I think I broke all the bones."

Grym didn't reply. I lifted my gaze to find him.

He was standing in the center of the huge space, hands on hips, looking around.

I rolled over and shoved gingerly to my feet. "What is this place?" Pain tweaked down my spine and through my hips when I tried to walk. Instead of exacerbating it, I dropped inelegantly to the flattish surface of a big rock, letting my gaze slide around the space. It was an enormous cavern, filled with odd-looking formations that rose from the floor, rounded and smooth as if they'd been manually shaped.

The eerie light I'd noticed in the vertical tunnel glowed softly from the formations and along the ground near the rock walls.

A high-pitched cackle brought my head up as Hobs swung past on a thick, hairy-looking vine and let go, flying through the air until he snagged a second vine and swung off into the shadows. "Hobs! Come down here. You have no idea what you're going to run into up there."

A beat later, he reappeared high above Grym's head, a thick, scaly vine clutched in his spidery fingers.

Slanted silver eyes glowered down at me as the "vine" uncoiled from a formation of rock and landed with a meaty "thump" right behind Grym. Hobs flew away with a gleeful sound as the snake hit the ground, rolling across the mossy floor.

"Watch out!" I screamed as the monstrous reptile

struck, fangs as long as my hands slamming into the ground inches from Grym.

The snake's muscular body retracted, its head lifting off the ground, and it snapped toward Hobs, venom dripping from its terrifying fangs.

"Run!" I screamed.

Grym reached over and snagged a giggling Hobs around the waist, turning to run.

The snake slammed its huge form down in front of them, cutting off their escape. In desperation, I picked up the biggest rock I could find and hurtled toward the monster, the rock poised above my head for maximum damage.

Grym dove to the side, flinging Hobs ahead of him and rolling as the snake struck again, fangs snapping like a junkyard dog.

Grym grunted in pain and I panicked, flinging the rock toward the snake's meaty coil.

It hit and bounced, pinging off into the shadows.

For a beat, I thought the snake was going to ignore my measly assault, but then its head snapped up, and the terrifying silver gaze slid in my direction.

A disgusting forked tongue slid out on an aggressive hiss.

I just stood there, immobilized with terror.

"Naida!" Grym yelled. He threw another rock at the monster, scoring a hit on its thick body. The thing's head whipped around, tail lifting as it considered striking at Grym.

"Run!" Grym screamed again.

And then it was too late. The thick, meaty body lashed out, wrapping around me before I could move away, and I was suddenly screaming as it yanked me toward the impenetrable shadows above.

Grym took a running leap and hit the snake just below the head, too near the snapping jaws for the fangs to find him. He wrapped his big body around the thick snake and held on as it whipped back and forth, trying to shake him off.

My stomach roiled as I was whipped back and forth with him, my brain sloshing painfully around in my skull.

In desperation, I pounded on the thing's coils, digging my nails into it in the hopes it would let me go. But I was like a mosquito trying to bite into a rhinoceros' hide.

A pale, skinny form whipped past and Hobs cackled gleefully as he flew over the snake and disappeared down the other side.

The crazy hobgoblin was playing while Grym and I fought for our lives.

A beat later, he flew past again, grinning widely at me as he rode the vine he was clutching over the snake again.

That's when it finally sank in. I looked at the vines twisting around the mammoth reptile's thick form and realized what Hobs was doing.

"Grym!" I yelled, jerking my head toward Hobs as he flew past once more, cackling happily.

Grym nodded and redoubled his efforts to keep the snake distracted. With its attention focused in three different directions, the snake's coils loosened slightly around my body.

I struggled to get free of them, knowing it would probably be an ugly and painful dismount if I did.

But the alternative was even uglier. I'd rather be bruised and sore than become snake kibble.

"Yippee!" Hobs screamed as he flew past the snake's head, barely avoiding the snapping jaws. His momentum swung him around the head like a lasso, the thick, hairy vine wrapping around the jaw and finally sealing it shut.

Grym wasted no time climbing toward the snout and, with a nod toward Hobs, rearing back and punching the snake right between the eyes.

Hobs released the vine and flew toward me, picking up another hanging vine on his way. He landed on the coils close to me as the snake's head wobbled a few times, and it started to fall.

"Grab hold, Miss," the hobgoblin screamed. I wrapped my arms around him and my legs around the vine as the coil released me, and we slid rapidly toward the ground.

Grym slid down the snake's body and leaped sideways before he was crushed beneath it.

He crawled to his feet and looked at us. "Everybody all right?"

I nodded, panting from adrenaline. "We're fine."

"Good." Grym pointed to a dark break in the rock wall that I hadn't noticed before. "We need to get out of here. I've been looking around, and that looks like the only potential way out."

I narrowed my gaze on the dark opening. "How do you know it leads out?"

Grym took a final look at the snake and started toward the cave. "I don't. But we're lean on choices. And we need to get away from that thing."

Hobs shot past, eager for the next adventure. I fell into step with Grym. I wanted to argue. To tell him the chances of that small opening giving us a way out were slim to none. And to tell him I was worried that we would run into something even worse than the giant snake. But I didn't say any of those things.

Because Grym was right. The opening was a chance. Probably the only one we had.

And I'd rather keep moving forward than stand still and give up.

Especially when standing still meant dealing with the monstrous snake that was already starting to wake up behind us.

19

HOLY GODDESS ON A THIGH MASTER!

T he air in the tunnel felt strange. Almost alive against my skin. The walls shimmered with something I couldn't quite see. The constant movement was making me jumpy.

And then there were the voices.

"Did you hear that?" I asked Grym.

He sent me a twitchy gaze, the shadows filling the curves and hollows of his handsome face and making them appear sharper, harder.

Like his gargoyle form.

"There's a low murmur," he agreed after a moment. "Like voices. But I can't understand anything they're saying."

I nodded in agreement.

Hobs was walking beside me, his spidery fingers wrapped tightly around mine. That alone was enough to give me the heebie-jeebies. The hobgoblin was never afraid.

The green squish wearing the tiny six-shooters was clutched in one of my hands, peeing and goddess knew what else on my palm. Occasionally he gave a soft, strangled-sounding croak to remind me that he wasn't happy there.

We rounded a tight curve and something flashed past, cold moisture seeping through my skin at its touch.

I jumped and shuddered. "Was that a ghost?"

Hobs wrapped himself around me, all but climbing my leg.

Grym didn't respond. His gaze was scouring the tunnel, his muscles taut. Had he gotten bigger?

The sharp scent of ozone filled my nostrils and I sneezed. Beneath my feet, the ground felt suddenly spongy and soft. It rolled away from my sensible flats like waves on the beach, making it hard to keep my balance.

A hiss slid through the tunnel, along with a shooshing sound that sounded all too much like an enormous snake slithering along the passage behind us.

In unspoken agreement, we picked up the pace, nearly running through the strange passageway.

The walls of the passage pulsed around us. Slithery white forms oozed in and out of the rock, sliding over us and leaving behind a cold sliminess that dripped along our skin. Hobs was shivering so hard *my* teeth were clacking from his quaking.

Okay, maybe the clacking teeth were from my own shivering. But I was a frog's hair away from giving in to my fear and assuming the fetal position in a corner.

If I could only find a corner.

I shoved my shoulders straight, digging deep in the search for my spine. If I didn't stay strong, I'd be drooling on myself and babbling incoherently in the blink of an eye.

Grym threw out an arm that felt like a mini-rock wall and I made an "umph" sound as I slammed into it. "Don't move," he whispered, his gaze locked on the tunnel ahead of us.

I followed his gaze and sucked in a gasp.

The floor of the tunnel was still moving. I'd almost gotten used to that. Unfortunately, the cause of the movement was no longer indiscernible.

"Are those..." I swallowed hard. "...snakes?"

Holy goddess on a thigh master! Drooling, gibberish-laden fetal position, here I come!

Hobs made a small sound of terror and I was suddenly wearing him like a scarf. I hunched my shoulders against the pain of pulled hair and lifted Slimy to my face. I wasn't sure why I lifted him, but elevation seemed just the thing when one had a friend who was a frog in a room full of snakes.

"Grym..."

He quaked...a violent quiver that ran from his head to his toes. His arm against my belly felt like rock.

I looked down. It was rock! "Grym, you shifted!"

He looked down too, holding his blocky, rock hands in front of his face. Frowning thoughtfully, he said, "Apparently, our magic works down here."

I didn't hesitate, flinging out a hand, I sent a ribbon of Keeper magic into the tunnel, and was rewarded by an immediate chime.

A beat later, something flew down the tunnel, heading right for me. I started to duck, not having any hands free to catch it, but Grym's big hand shot up and he caught the bag before it collided with my face.

He held the small, gold clutch in front of me. "Well, at least you'll be dressed for success."

I sighed. "Why can't I ever get anything useful when I use my magic?"

Grym chuckled. "The good thing is that rock is impermeable to snake fangs." He eyed Hobs. "Let me take him and the frog through. Then I'll come back for you."

I nodded, handing him the frog.

Trickle, trickle, trickle.

The gargoyle grimaced. "Ugh!"

Sorry man. I'm scared.

Grym and I shot Slimy a look. He'd spoken!

I smiled. "I heard you!"

The frog shifted slightly on Grym's palm. *There's magic in this place*, he told us. *Not like up above.*

His words spurred a niggling thought that I couldn't quite grasp. "Can you look ahead and see what kind of magic is waiting for us?" I asked the little green guy.

There's a mix, He said. *Good magics and really bad energy. It's all mixed up. Like somebody opened a hole in the earth and dumped it all down here together.*

I looked at Grym. That was exactly what had happened. The artifact had stripped everybody's magic, along with their ability to defend themselves, and dumped it in the caverns where we stood.

It was a thought that needed further exploration. But first we had to get out of that snake-filled tunnel.

"Are those snakes real?" Grym asked the frog.

They look real to me, sayeth the frog. *And those aren't normal snakes. They're fast and agile. They can jump.*

Judging by the bulging aspect of his black eyes, I believed him.

The hiss behind us slid through the tunnel like a physical presence, still a distance away but closing the gap too quickly. In front of us, the writhing mass of undulating snakiness grew more agitated, the tendrils of the mass slithering out in different directions, like an ugly slinking star.

Several of them were headed for us.

I swallowed hard, one part of my brain locked on

the sough, sough, soughing of a heavy reptile form sliding through the curves of the passageway behind us. "Get Hobs and Slimy out," I told Grym. "I'll see what I've got in this bag that might help me."

Brave words, spoken in a breathy, terrified voice that hadn't fooled anybody.

Grym wrapped his rocky fingers around my arm, squeezing more gently than I'd have thought possible with such digits. He lowered his head and looked down on me with a warm, caramel gaze. "I'll be back for you, Naida. I promise."

I nodded, not really believing him, and stepped away, forcing him to move. "Go."

It took a bit to unclench Hobs from my leg. He looked up at me with a terrified blue gaze. "You come too, Miss."

I reached out and tugged on the light brown hair that spiked adorably from between his oversized ears. Somewhere along the line, not too surprisingly, the little guy had lost his cowboy hat. "I'll be right behind you, buddy. I promise."

My throat closed on that promise. I wasn't sure if it was a lie. Or if I'd really find a way to get to them before the monster behind me or the pile of mini-monsters in front of me made their move.

I looked away as Grym plucked him from my leg and tucked him against his side, one arm holding him under the bum like a toddler. "Be careful," I told them.

Handing Slimy to Hobs, Grym didn't move for a moment, his big body a warm, solid comfort inches away.

I looked up into his face, seeing the fear reflected in his gaze, and reached for him, my hand finding his cheek and pressing. "I'll be fine."

"Maybe I could carry you too."

I was tempted but I thought about how heavy Hobs was. He looked small and wiry but in the way of magical things, his weight was deceptive. And Grym was going to need a hand free to fight off snakes. I shook my head. "No. That wouldn't work. Go. I'll be fine." I held up the artifact I'd called. "This is here for a reason. Maybe it's got something that will help us get out of here. I'll be right behind you, I promise."

Grym pressed his cheek against my palm and sighed. "I'll be back as fast as I can."

I nodded.

He turned away and headed for the mass of writhing snakes. I shuddered at the sight of them all slithering out to attack. Hobs hid his face in Grym's shoulder and Slimy croaked in alarm.

My pulse shot sky-high with worry for them.

Several snakes flew off the ground and hit Grym's chest, fangs snapping toward Hobs and Slimy.

Grym's free hand snatched them off his chest and slammed them against the wall, kicking out at the next group of attacking reptiles and rushing through the opening he'd created.

In desperation, I tugged the small bag open and looked inside, hoping it was one of those never-ending stuff purses. I'd picked up one of those recently in a neutral dimension, and it had come in handy fighting off demons.

However, all the little purse contained was a single, folded tissue, a small flashlight, and a key. I reached inside and grabbed the key, pulling it out to examine. It was one of those old-fashioned skeleton keys, as long as my hand and heavy. The metal was tarnished almost to black and felt warm against my palm.

A sibilant sound danced through the funky passage and ice formed on my spine. The snake was coming. It sounded close.

I turned toward the spot in the passage where Grym had been. He and his passengers were gone. Unfortunately, not all the snakes had followed them down the tunnel.

They writhed along the floor en masse, and they were even more agitated than before. With a collective hiss of rage, the whole mess of the things boiled toward me, tongues tasting the air. Angry hissing tugged the small hairs up along my arms.

In desperation, I swung out a hand and sent my power into them, a dull silver wash of energy that shot from my fingers with more power than I'd expected, no doubt fueled by my fear.

The energy hit the first wave of snakes and yanked them off the ground, spinning them on the air. As I swung my arm, the magic slammed them against the wall as Grym had done.

The next wave split up, coming at me from several directions at once. It would be harder to stop them all at once, leaving the ones I missed to attack while I was busy.

Smart snakes. Just my luck.

Regurgitated Reptile spit!

I painted the floor with my energy, giving it everything I had as they bubbled and writhed inside the deadly silver wave.

To my great relief, the rest of the snakes retreated, slithering around the curve in the passageway and disappearing.

Hopefully, Grym and the kids were well along the passage and beyond their threat.

I stood there a long moment, trying to see into the shadows ahead to see if it was safe for me to pass.

The light was too dull. The shadows too deep.

Inspiration struck. I reached into the purse I was still clutching like a lifeline and pulled out the small flashlight. I turned it on and slid it along the spot where the snakes had been. There was movement on the edges of the arc of light, but no snakes appeared in the illuminated area.

I took a deep breath and released it, trying to relax. I stood there a moment, considering whether I wanted to move forward or wait for Grym.

The coward in me wanted to wait.

My pride told me I needed to save myself. I didn't need the gargoyle to save me.

Not much anyway.

A cool, meaty scent slid over me, spiking the hairs on the back of my neck. Dread and sudden realization made me go perfectly still.

I listened, scented the air, and felt the magic biting gently against my skin.

A wisp of my hair blew away from my cheek, the breeze smelling like a butcher shop.

Shoosh, shoosh, shoosh...

The soft shooshing sound made me close my eyes as terror turned my limbs to lead. "No, no, no, no..." I whispered softly, knowing what I'd see when I turned.

Something dripped to the ground behind me. The soft plop of liquid splashed acid against my bare ankle.

Agony seared through my flesh where the drop burned. I forced myself not to move, certain I'd be dead if I did.

Clutching the tiny flashlight between my fingers, I took a deep breath, said a prayer to the goddess that I'd survive the next few seconds, and slowly turned, stabbing the darkness with the bright arc of the flash.

Slanted silver eyes peered down on me. Fangs as long as my hand hovered on the air two feet away, the slitted nostrils scenting me through the musty air. The tongue snapped out, tasting the air only inches from my face.

Sizzling snake snot!

I shuddered, my fingers nearly dropping the flashlight, and opened my mouth to scream.

The monster reared back, its massive jaws opening wide, and then snapped its head in my direction, massive fangs flinging venom into the air as it attacked.

20

THERE'S NO NEED TO DISRESPECT
THE FROG

I dived sideways, crashing into the side of the tunnel as the fangs snapped together inches away. I scrabbled backward as fast as I could but the snake kept pace, jaw snapping in an attempt to impale me on its fangs.

I flung myself into a roll a heartbeat before the fangs sank deep into the ground where I'd been. Climbing to my feet, I started to run. The snake struck again, its massive head slamming into me and sending me flying on a yelp of pain. I landed where the mass of smaller snakes had been, the ground slimy with something I didn't want to examine too closely.

The monster snake uncoiled and it was suddenly on top of me again, its snout an inch from my nose. I pressed back as far as I could go, hitting the wall way too soon.

Venom dripped, sizzling ominously over the ground near my feet.

I gave a small sound of pure fear, my throat closing around it, and my heart trying to beat its way through my ribs. Bracing myself against the wall, I watched in horror as the enormous jaws slowly opened, my death mirrored in the slanted silver eyes.

My hand hit something cool and metallic on the ground. I trailed my fingers over it, realizing it was the flashlight. In desperation, I wrapped my fingers around the metal tool, thinking I could at least jam it between the snake's jaws when it tried to bite down.

It was a weak plan, fraught with so many possible problems. But it was all I had.

I was pretty sure the key and the tissue in the purse would be worthless against a snake that was easily fifty feet long.

The snake's thick form tensed, shifted slightly, and I knew what it was going to do even before the huge head snapped forward.

With a scream of pure terror, I lifted the flashlight, my thumb grazing over a lever on the side I hadn't known was there. A wash of pale pink light flared over the snake a beat before its strike slammed home.

The strike never came.

I blinked, watching the silver eyes widen slightly in surprise, and then took the opportunity to scramble away. The pink arc of light wrapped itself around the monster, pulling him into the air and wringing him down to nothing.

The snake disappeared with a pop and a burst of pink energy.

I shoved slowly to my feet, pain enveloping me as adrenaline slowly eased out of my muscles.

I glanced down at the flashlight in my hand, realizing it had somehow saved me.

I looked to the spot where the snake had disappeared, squinting as the ground seemed to shift and wiggle.

It was still there! But it was tiny, and I could barely see it. Apparently, it still existed on a microscopic level.

A temporary fix?

I wouldn't wait around to find out.

Shaking my head, I carefully slid my thumb back over the lever that had engaged the pink energy and gathered up my things. As I reached for the fallen purse, pain slashed through my arm. I looked down to find a long, ragged tear in the skin of my forearm where a fang had evidently scored a hit. As soon as I noticed it, the wound burned and throbbed. I stumbled a bit as panic flared. "What if there was poison in its venom?" I mumbled to myself.

Blood oozed from the wound and slid down my arm. The blood burned where it touched my skin, probably from the venom mixed into it.

I reached inside the bag and grabbed the tissue. Leaning against the cool wall, I wiped the wound, wincing at the agony of touching it.

But wiping off the venom made it feel better almost immediately. I shoved the bloodied tissue back into the bag along with the flashlight and made sure the key was still there. Then I set off down the passage, hoping to catch up to Grym before any more monsters found me.

Given my track record so far of escaping "all the bad things," I was pretty sure that wouldn't be happening.

I found a tiny gun holster and hat on the ground several yards ahead in the passage. Frowning, I hoped that didn't mean the boys had run into more trouble. I slipped the items into my purse in case Slimy wanted them back, and plowed onward.

After an hour had passed without an end to the passageway or any sign of Grym and the boys, I started to worry. "Can this stupid passage really be this long?" I complained to myself. And why hadn't I run into Grym? He should have been able to tuck Hobs and Slimy safely into a nook somewhere and come back.

Worry tightened my chest and sped my steps. As

I moved along the seemingly endless tube of rock and dirt, I became more and more convinced they'd found trouble.

If that was the case, I was probably the only one who could help. I doubted there were any other rebels in the underground cave and tunnel system we'd literally fallen into.

My pulse spiked. My heart rate sped. After trying to calm myself for several minutes without success, I finally gave into my panic and started to run.

The passage ended without warning. One second I was flying along in a near panic, huffing and blowing like a water buffalo, and the next I was standing in another cavern, smaller than the first but still a good size. Like the previous cavern, it was filled with the strange formations, the eerie green light filling the space with dubious light.

I looked frantically around, panic flaring brighter when I didn't see my friends.

"Grym? Hobs?"

Silence met my call, and a deep feeling of foreboding filled me.

Something was wrong.

Something was *very* wrong.

A tiny form appeared in the center of the cave. I

squinted through the soft green light and realized it was Mr. Slimy. He was naked as I'd known he would be, and he wasn't talking to me.

For a moment, I wondered if it was a different frog. But it looked too much like him and he kept hopping in my direction, bulging black gaze locked on me.

"Slimy?" I tried again.

The frog hopped right up to me and landed on my foot. I looked down, perplexed. "Slimy, is that you?"

Hush! sayeth the frog. *We don't want him to know I'm anything but a normal frog.*

I had no idea who *He* was, but I decided to play along. Flinging up my arms, I said, "Argh! It's a nasty, warty frog!"

I could feel Slimy rolling his eyes in my head. *There's no need to disrespect the frog*, he said.

What's going on? I asked. *Where are Grym and Hobs?*

He has them. Slimy took a hop onto my other shoe. I really hoped nothing scared him. Frog pee trickling down into my shoe was an experience I never wanted to have.

He, who? Sheriff Andrew?

"Hi," a sweet, young voice said from across the cavern.

I looked up to find Opie standing between two of the formations, small hands shoved into the pockets of his rough pants and his thick hair falling into his eyes. As I looked at him, his form wavered slightly and the air between the formations sizzled with light.

I blinked and he was whole again, the air clear.

I squeezed my eyes tight and then opened them, giving him a smile. "Hey, Opie. Is your dad around?"

Run, Slimy told me, hopping off my foot. *Get behind a rock or something.*

I ignored him, taking a step toward the little boy.

Opie smiled. "Pa's not here. He's lookin' for some bad guys." Opie cocked his head. "You ain't one of them bad guys, is ya?"

"No. Of course not," I told him, laughing. I took another step in his direction, drawn in by the clear blue gaze and adorable freckles. "I was just looking for my friends. Have you seen them?"

Naida, you need to take cover. Something's building behind the boy. Something ugly.

I turned to Slimy, frowning. *Is he in danger?*

Slimy was silent. I took that as a yes. I moved closer still. "What are you doing down here, Opie? It's not a safe place for little boys to play."

I immediately realized my mistake. His little face folded into a thunder cloud. "I ain't little."

Holding up my hands in supplication, I smiled. "Sorry, that didn't come out right. You're definitely not little. But I'm guessing your pa wouldn't like that you're down here. Would he?"

Opie's frown slid away. "He ain't gonna know about it. He's busy like always. I like ta come down here and play." His form wavered again as if he were only a hologram. But when he went solid, I could tell he was every bit as real as I was. He smiled, showing me crooked teeth. "Pa don't know I found the door into this place. Only he has the key."

Well, that certainly put a ticky mark in the column for Sheriff Andrew being our artifact gate-keeper. Or, as Dugan would say, the heart of the artifact.

"Have you seen my friends down here?" I asked again.

Opie turned his head and pointed toward a nearby wall. I gasped.

Grym and Hobs were hanging high above our heads, wrapped in vines like the ones Hobs had been swinging on in the other cavern. Their bodies were limp and their heads drooped.

Suddenly, Slimy's lost cowboy costume made more sense. They hadn't wanted *him*, whoever *he* was, to know Slimy was magical. They'd been counting on the little green squish to warn me.

And I'd ignored his warnings.

Holy hoppin' heartache! I was a derf.

Still, I couldn't just leave a small boy in danger. Not if there was even the smallest chance I could help him. I moved close enough to grab Opie's arm. "I was wondering if you'd come over there, near my friends with me. Maybe you can help me figure out how to get them down."

If they're still alive.

The random thought impaled my poor, delicate heart like one of the Indian's spears.

I shook it off as soon as I thought it. They had to be alive. Rationally, there would be no need to hang them above the cavern if they were already dead.

Emotionally...well...I'd fought off a monster snake and possibly poisoned myself on venom to get to them. I didn't want to believe I might have lost them anyway.

Besides, I'd miss Hobs' irrepressible *joie de vivre* and Grym's...

Well, Grym's everything.

Opie shrugged and I reached out, offering him my hand. He took it with childish trust and I pulled him gently away from the formations.

He stepped away from the eerily lit rocks just in time.

Naida! Get out of there, now! Slimy screamed in my head.

The cavern rumbled, rock dust sifting down from high above our heads. I started to run but the floor beneath my feet split apart and I was forced to jump or find myself falling down the crack.

Opie's hand slipped away from mine as the floor fell out from under me, and it was all I could do to grab the edge before I was sucked down into it.

I hung on with everything I had, but I had zero strength in my arms. I hadn't done a single pushup or pullup in my life. The idea that I could hold the result of hundreds of brownies and egg rolls up as the ground continued to shake and the cavern to rumble was ridiculous.

Still, I had no choice. It was hold or die.

An icy wind swirled upward from the crack, stale and putrid with the smell of old, dark magic.

The color we'd regained from falling into the caverns was washed away under the putrid touch of the magic, turning us all shades of black and white again.

With a horrified start of surprise, I realized I'd found the heart of the thing. And it was angry. So angry, that I was there.

I kicked at the jagged rock under my stupid girly shoes, feeling the toe catch finally but the shoe threaten to slip off my foot. In desperation, I shook my foot and let the shoe fall into the abyss yawning below me. Then I dug my toes into the rock and, functioning under sheer desperation, shoved myself upward a few inches.

My fingers scrabbled ineffectually against the rocky cavern floor, unable to catch enough to sustain my weight. I started to slip down again. Screaming my frustration, I dug my feet into the rock and pushed.

Muscles screamed and tore. Agony blossomed

through me as my fingertips ripped, turning slippery with blood.

I fought tears, knowing I was the only one who could save Grym and the others, but also knowing I wasn't up to the challenge.

I was going to fail. And they were going to die.

Then I remembered the purse. I'd shoved it into the waistband of my skirt when I'd been running down the passageway looking for my friends. Unfortunately, there was no way I could reach it without letting go with one hand. And I wasn't letting go.

I was barely holding on as it was.

But there was something...

Closing my eyes, I fought to concentrate on pulling the magic forward, knowing it would be a miracle if I managed it under the blanket of stress and fear currently covering me.

I thought of the object I wanted to call.

The magic hit with the force of a freight train. And when it flew from my fingers, it nearly blew me right off the wall I was clinging to.

I screamed, clutching the wall with every ounce of desperation in my soul.

Panting from my efforts, I tried climbing upward again, managing to tug myself an inch farther up the rock wall before I slid down again.

The cavern finally quieted, the ground ceasing its constant rolling beneath me, and I took a deep breath.

I jolted in surprise as the object I'd called clattered loudly to the floor mere inches away.

It had worked!

Elation filled me. Followed quickly by despair. If I tried to reach for the pitchfork I'd called, I'd surely fall. There was no way I could grab it before my single stick arm gave out and sent me plunging.

"Blithering bat boogers!" I screamed into the cavern.

A soft, distant giggling reminded me that I wasn't alone. My head jerked upward. "Opie? Opie, I need your help."

Feet shuffled against the cavern floor behind me.

I realized he might not be able to get to me. Even if he wanted to. He'd probably ended up on the opposite side and I had no idea how far the crack ran. "Can you get to this pitchfork?" I asked him, not hopeful.

Silence.

No help from that quarter. Fortunately, I hadn't really expected any. I'd have to figure it out on my own.

Without warning, I slid backward several inches. I yelped, barely managing to dig my toes into the wall to keep from falling.

I took deep breaths, in danger of hyperventilating if I didn't get my panic under control. I risked a glance upward, finding Grym and Hobs still hanging limply above me.

Even if I could rouse them, I doubted they'd be able to peel the vining away and get to me.

Not in time, anyway.

Despair swept through me. I looked at the pitch-fork and tried to pull more energy into my fingertips.

Nothing.

I stretched my fingers toward the fork, realizing I was inches too far away. The only way I'd be able to get to it would be to lunge for it and get my grip on the rock again before I fell.

It would be a delicate balance of timing. I doubted I could pull it off.

No! I shook off the negative thought. I *could* do it. I had no choice.

"Ribbit!"

I looked up to find Slimy hopping onto the upturned tines of the fork. I opened my mouth to yell at him, but the shaft lifted from his weight. He hopped to one side and the shaft shifted closer.

I wanted to scream in joy. "Slimy, you're a genius."

He hopped again, and again, until the handle was close enough to my fingers to grab. I pressed my fingers over it and Slimy jumped off. *You'll need to brace it*, he told me.

I risked turning my head enough to see the crevice. I couldn't turn far without slipping away from the wall. My grip was too tenuous. "What do you mean?"

Brace it across the crevice, he said, his tone impatient.

I shook my head. "I have no idea how wide the crack is. I don't know if this is long enough."

It's your only chance, he said, hopping closer.

"I just don't think..." The cavern rumbled and roared, rocks plummeting from the ceiling high above, and my fingers slipped from the wall.

With a shrill scream of pure terror, I started to fall.

21

TRICKLE, TRICKLE, TRICKLE...

My arms shot out, clutching in desperation for anything I could find, and closed around the shaft of the pitchfork. It slid off the flat surface and I grabbed frantically for it, even as I realized it was too short to hold me at the top of the crack.

I fell a couple of feet and then slammed to a stop as the shaft wedged into the sides. The crack was narrower a few feet from the top.

Thank the goddess.

I yelped as my shoulders were nearly pulled from their sockets. But I was still alive.

Wasting no time, I wrapped my arms around the shaft and walked my feet up the wall until I could roll over the handle, draped along my belly. I paused briefly to breathe away a wave of panic. Forcing myself not to look down, I shimmied toward the opposite side.

I just needed to get to the wall so I could climb...

A loud cracking sound filled the air. I yelped and shoved against the shaft with one foot, propelling me toward the other side as fast as I could go. When I got close enough to reach the wall, I gave the pitchfork handle one last shove with my feet and launched myself past the edge.

I barely hit the rocky edge before the pitchfork cracked completely in half and fell away, disappearing into the vast emptiness below.

I hit the hard dirt with the top half of my body, knocking the wind from my lungs. I shoved at the rocky wall and managed to get my whole body onto flat ground, then lay there for a moment, my heart pounding. After a moment, I sat up, shoving hair out of my face.

I looked across the crevice.

And nearly emptied my bladder, Slimy style.

Trickle, trickle, trickle.

Mouth hanging open and heart still slamming against my ribs, I was dimly aware of a soft sound down by my feet and a squishy weight on my shoe.

I really don't like the looks of that, said the frog.

I really didn't either. "Is that a...worm?"

Slimy only swallowed hard.

I couldn't blame him. "I hate worms. They're disgusting." And that whole whacking them in half and making two worms out of one thing is just weird. I especially didn't like them when they were as big around as a small car.

I slammed my mouth closed and swallowed copious amounts of spit. "What are we going to do with that?" I asked the frog.

For starters, let's not make it mad.

I couldn't help it. I snorted out a laugh. Worms had a lot to be mad about. First of all, there's that whole fishing thing. Not good for the worm. Not even a little bit. And then there's gardening. I glanced down to the frog on my shoe. "Do you know how many worms I've accidentally hacked into pieces planting stuff in my garden?"

Ixnay on the ackinghay, Slimy muttered. *That's not the way to keep it from getting mad.*

We stared silently at the monster-sized annelid. I blinked, amazed I remembered that from science classes. I remembered the weirdest stuff. And generally forgot anything useful. "What do worms eat?" I asked the frog.

If he could have shrugged, I was pretty sure he would have. *When they're the size of a car, whatever they want.*

I narrowed my gaze at the slimy creature, which seemed to have chunks of black dirt pasted along its greasy length. "Can it see us?"

We could try running for our lives and see, suggested the frog.

Running sounded like a really good idea. But

then I remembered Grym and Hobs, still hanging on the wall. "We can't. We need to help the others."

The worm shifted suddenly. Its *head?* lifted off the ground and waved back and forth as if trying to sense something. I slowly bent down and scooped up Slimy. We started to back away from the massive worm, toward the wall where Hobs and Grym hung quiet and limp. I had no idea how I was going to help them. But doing it quickly had just become imperative.

The worm's front half slammed back to the ground, shaking the cavern so hard I stumbled and fell. I hit the ground hard with my knees, and my teeth clacked painfully on impact. The worm was suddenly sliding over the crack, its massive body easily bridging it.

I wanted to believe it was simply slithering around, blind, but its movement seemed all too fixated on me for comfort.

You might want to start running, sayeth the bossy frog.

I forgave him his bossiness because of the hysterical edge to his voice. I shoved to my feet with my free hand and took off running. Moving slowly hadn't done any good. And, though there was likely no way I was going to outrun the thing, I had to try.

Grym and Hobs hung several feet above my head. There was one of those eerily lit rock formations nearby and, though I was hesitant to touch it, not knowing what kind of magic it involved, I didn't see any other options. I settled Slimy between the formation and the wall, thinking the worm wouldn't be able to see or get to him there. "Wait here," I told him. "I need to see if I can get them down."

The frog didn't argue, which spoke volumes for how scared he was.

I moved over to the glowy rock, reaching out and giving it a tentative tap with a finger to test it for heat.

It was warmish but not hot. I tried notching a foot into a niche in the side and pulling myself up, testing it for the ability to hold my weight. I didn't know if the things were some kind of lantern, in which case they might not be very sturdy. Or just special, glowing rocks.

It felt sturdy, so I shoved upward, resting my palms against the wall to steady myself on the rounded top.

Behind me, a meaty swooshing sound told me the worm was on the move again.

There was also a low, rhythmic hum that might have been coming from the slimy monster. Or, it might have been coming from the lighted rock beneath me. In the cavern, sound had a funny way of sliding around, its origin confused.

I tried to ignore the encroaching nightmare and reached for Grym's foot. He was still in his gargoyle form, and his eyes were closed, his chin resting on his chest. What had the artifact done to him? It was like he'd been put into some kind of stasis.

Swoosh, swoosh, swoosh...

I glanced at Hobs and gave a yelp of surprise. His blue eyes were open, and they were filled with fear.

Not asleep. Only immobilized. Was Grym awake too?

I tugged on Grym's blocky foot. "Grym, if you can hear me, you need to fight this. There's a massive worm in here and he's coming after us."

Swoosh, swoosh, swoosh...

Naida? the frog said, sounding nervous.

Grym's foot twitched slightly in my hand, and a clump of black dirt sifted off him as a result of the movement.

I looked at the dirt laying on my hand, feeling a strange numbness that didn't bode well. I realized with a start that the dirt was a numbing agent. Was that what had happened to Grym and Hobs? Had they been covered in the black dirt? The dirt was sticky and I couldn't rub it off. In desperation, I tugged the small purse from my waistband and pulled it open, reaching inside for the tissue.

I blinked as my fingers found it, pulling it out.

It was perfectly clean and tidily folded again. As if I'd never used it to wipe blood off my arm. Weird. And really good. Because it meant the tissue was a magical artifact.

I scrubbed at the black dirt and, to my relief, it came off. The numbness started to fade.

Staring at it for a moment, I realized what I needed to do.

I reached up and wiped the tissue along Grym's leg. I ran it quickly over his foot and up to one knee. Then I started on the other leg.

Naida! Slimy screamed behind me. *"Watch out!"*

The rock I was standing on shook as the thick, slimy form of the worm slammed into it. I screamed as I fell, smacking into the greasy body and sliding off onto the ground.

The skin of my body where it had touched the worm turned numb. I half crawled, half dragged myself into the crevice where I'd hidden Slimy.

"Don't let it touch you," I told the frog. I looked around for the tissue, which I'd dropped when the worm smacked into the rock.

I found the magical tissue near my foot, but my fingers wouldn't work. The whole side of my body was completely limp.

The worm slammed into the rock again and I screamed. The formation above our heads cracked and the top two-thirds of it went askew. One more good hit and it was going to land on top of me. The worm wouldn't need to make me numb. I'd be dead from the weight of the fallen rock.

I had to do something. Fast.

There was only one thing I could do. And, like

everything else I'd tried, I had no idea if it would work. I lifted the fingers of my good hand and, filling my mind with the item I needed, sent a jolt of keeper magic into the air.

I watched it swirl away, sucking in a breath as it nearly got caught on the writhing monster above me. After a brief, terrifying hesitation, the magic shot away from the worm and disappeared through a ragged spot in the cavern wall on the other side of the crevice.

I closed my eyes and prayed it would work.

If it didn't, my friends and I would never make it out of the poisonous black and white artifact.

Even as I had the thought, the worm reared up and swung its huge body into the rock wall where Grym and Hobs hung. Rock shards rained down on us, dust filled my nose and stung my eyes. I tugged Slimy close with my good hand and tried to wrap myself around him, praying salvation would arrive in time.

22

GAH! HAVE YE LOST YER BLEEPIN' MIND?

Somehow I managed not to die. And, as a meaty "thump" hit the ground near my head, I recognized Hobs' muffled exclamation as he hit. I shoved upward as much as I could to look at him. I didn't get far. My body was still almost completely numb on one side. Worse, I was bleeding along my arm and something was running into my eyes. When the numbness gave way, I was pretty sure it was gonna hurt like the dickens.

Some of the dust shifted and Slimy hopped out of it, the tissue stuck on his tongue. He hopped over to my hand. *Here. We need to get out of here, fast.*

He wasn't wrong.

But I was hoping the reinforcements I'd just called would get there soon and help us with the worm. I had no idea why, but I was sure the secret to defeating the artifact was in that cavern. And I was determined to find it.

I clasped the tissue with the tips of my fingers and tugged it out of the frog's mouth. *Ew!* There were probably fly legs stuck to it. I rubbed it against my numb hand and arm, slowly feeling the numbness ease as I moved the tissue over it.

When I could move again, I took a beat to peek over the rock at the worm and found it about twenty feet away, unmoving.

Maybe it was resting after all its work.

Or not. Upon closer examination, I spotted a silvery shimmer spreading slowly toward us across the floor. I watched it spread, realizing it was coming from the worm. Since I was pretty sure I hadn't killed the monster with my mean thoughts, I figured that silvery stuff wasn't its lifeblood running out.

It was more likely bad news for us. I turned over onto my belly and army-crawled toward Hobs, quickly washing him with the tissue. His face, hands, and arms clear, he grabbed for me. "Miss! We can't let that wet stuff touch us. I saw it kill a bunch of snakes that it touched."

Well, that solved that riddle. I quickly rubbed his legs. "I need you to climb up there and use this to free Grym."

"But Miss, what about the big worm thing?" He pointed to the nasty annelid.

"I'll handle that, Hobs." I shoved the tissue at him. "Just get Grym free. I'll need his help."

He nodded and his eyes went wide as something whispered toward us through the air. Without even looking, I raised my hand and caught it, the warm, familiar hilt molding to my grip. A ball of tumbling feathers rolled across the cavern behind the sword, smacking into me and sending me to the ground with a mouthful of gray and black feathers.

I choked on the feathers and pushed the bird off my face. "Ugh! What's with the less than graceful entrance?" I asked SB the Parrot.

"Bwawk! Bloody bleep!" He clattered his wings and rose to a spot on the broken rock above my head, landing crooked and nearly falling over.

SB, short for Sewer Beak, was suffering under a magical bleeping spell because his language was so bad. That was what happened when one spent the years of one's life hanging around with a bunch of pirates.

"This be a bleepin' unlikely place, Lass. I think its broken me eyes."

I pushed to my knees, watching Hobs climb the wall like a spider and grasp the vines holding Grym to the wall. "Your eyes? What's wrong with them?"

"They be seeing in the colors of death. I can't live without me pirate colors, Lass."

The sword in my hand danced across the air as if

in agreement. I noted the monotone leather on the hilt where once it had been a warm, reddish-brown.

"It's a color leeching artifact, SB. We're trying to kill it."

The parrot lifted his wings and cocked his head, feathers rippling with pique. "It's a bleepin' bloody crisis, it is. Bwawk! A man shouldn't have his bleepin' identity torn asunder. It ain't bloody right."

I nodded, deciding not to tell him that his colors might return if he stayed long in the cavern. The magic there seemed to negate the color-bleaching quality of the artifact.

I nodded. "You'll be fine. Pull it together, parrot. I need your help with this giant worm thing." I eyed the silvery liquid that had spread a couple of feet closer than the last time I'd looked. Was it moving quicker? The stuff had all but cut off our escape route, sliming the ground between us and the worm and all the way to the crevice.

"Aye, Lass. What is it you'd like me ta do?"

"I don't suppose parrots eat worms?"

His whole body quivered with what looked like revulsion. "Gah! Have ye lost yer bleepin' mind? I'm a grog and pineapple man, make no mistake. Sides, yer forgettin' that I'm dead as a portal latch. I ain't eatin' nothing and I ain't lettin' nothing eat me."

"Well, aren't you helpful," I growled out.

Hobs landed beside me and the parrot flew upward with a squawk, grayish-black feathers painting the air around him. "Bloody bleep, ya blackguard! Ye've no more sense than a bosun with a short barrel of rum and a long straw!"

Hobs grinned widely. "Mr. SB, welcome to the bad place."

The parrot squawked again to show his annoyance.

The cavern shook under Grym's descent. He landed behind me in a crouch, his blocky fists bracing him on the floor. I couldn't help thinking he looked like a comic book hero when he did that.

The gargoyle lifted his dark-caramel gaze to mine. "Thanks for the rescue."

I thought he seemed sheepish about it. Probably because he'd been supposed to rescue me. "No worries, gargoyle. Giant worms happen."

His chuckle was a comfortable rumble in his rock-like chest. "What's the plan?"

The worm shifted, its pointy front half rising slightly as if it was sensing our conversation. From what I'd read about worms, I knew they had no eyes, perceiving rather than seeing through sensors in their bodies.

The silver shimmer on the floor was only a couple of feet away from us. Whatever we were going to do, we needed to do it fast. I glanced toward the crevice, sliding my gaze to the spot where my keeper magic had disappeared. "We need to get to the other side of the cavern," I told them, my tone filled with question.

Grym frowned at the oversized crack. "How'd that get there?"

"Long story," I told him.

"Ribbit!" agreed the frog.

I looked at Grym. "Can you jump it?"

"I can, Miss," Hobs said.

I wasn't surprised. Nodding, I arched a brow at Grym. I could tell from his hesitation that he wasn't sure he'd make it. His gargoyle form was heavy and strong, but not very agile.

"Maybe if I shifted back," he finally said.

I grimaced, knowing he'd be naked if he did. There were no magical boxer shorts under that rock-like facade. "Um, okay. That's one option."

Sensing my unease, Grym nodded toward the encroaching liquid. "That's not good. We stepped into something that looked like that earlier and woke up on the wall."

"We need to get away from it," I agreed, wondering if I'd called the wrong artifact.

The glowy green formations all flickered at once, the room pulsing with a sickly light.

Without warning, the worm reared up and charged right at us.

"Bwawk!" SB squawked loudly.

The worm's thick body shoved the lake of silver

liquid it had been making ahead of it as it hurtled in our direction.

"Off the ground!" I screamed, getting nearly decapitated as Hobs flew past me and landed on the broken formation. I grabbed Slimy and handed him to Hobs and then jumped up behind the hobgoblin.

My terrified gaze slid to Grym. I was relieved to see him standing on another formation. Relief left me a beat later as he leaped to another rock and then another, working his way around the worm's numbing magic.

"Grym!" I yelled, wondering what he was going to do.

In the next moment, I realized the old adage was true.

Ignorance really was bliss.

Grym's big feet hit the last rock and propelled him into the air. When he landed, he was sitting astride the worm. And my heart stopped beating.

The monster reared up, lifting its entire body off the ground and high, high into the cavern airspace.

Grym somehow held on, though I have no idea how he did it. The worm's body had zero places to hold onto. No bumps, no curves, and slimy to boot.

I grimaced even as I turned to SB. "Go help him!"

The parrot rose, outraged, into the air with a mighty squawk, but he beat his wings and took off toward the worm.

Hobs clasped my hand. "Hold on, Miss!"

The world tilted, shifted around me, and returned somewhere behind the shimmering poison on the ground. I wobbled on my feet, my head spinning for a beat, and then looked up at the worm. I was looking at Grym's back.

Turning to Hobs, I spiked my brows in surprise. "How'd you do that?"

He shrugged. "A space shift, Miss. I do them all the time."

I narrowed my gaze. "You run really fast. I didn't know you could actually shift space."

He nodded, and I realized he could probably get us over the crevice the same way.

High above us, Grym let out a grunt of pain and I looked up in horror as the worm rolled underneath him and snapped at him with its nasty mouth.

Shimmering silver spittle flew through the air. Grym was in danger of being coated with the stuff again.

I looked at Hobs. "We'll talk about this later."

The hobgoblin shrugged. I took off running, slamming to a stop alongside the worm's massive middle and slicing across it with the blade.

Nasty green blood oozed out and the worm bucked, silently writhing in pain.

Before I knew what was happening, the thing had flipped around, its mouth snapping mere inches from my head.

I jumped back, letting the sword have its full magic.

Above me, SB lunged and danced on the air, his dance mimicking the sword's movements. The parrot's high-pitched voice rang through the cavern as I swung the blade, spun away, and sliced again.

SB began the familiar refrain of the sword and I stepped into its rhythm.

"Ye might think ye'll know, ye might think ye'll see. But Blackbeard's blade will cleave to thee."

I flashed forward so quickly I didn't even have time to think about moving, the blade like a silver blur through the space.

The worm writhed and struck and writhed again, trying to fight the deadly battle we'd brought to it. Grym shoved to his feet and ran along the slimy, slippery form, rearing back with a massive fist and slamming it into the creature's body just beneath its mouth.

Something ripped inside the beast and more greenish blood ran from its maw.

The enormous body shuddered, crashing sideways and nearly taking me off my feet. But I was under the spell of the sword and I leaped above the slashing form, landing several feet away in a fighting crouch.

SB's wings throbbed on the air. He dropped to plunge knife-like talons into the worm's belly, drawing more blood from his attack. "Ye scurvy dog believe ye see. But you'll not track the blade. Not thee."

The blade slashed again, opening up a long, shallow cut that spilled more blood the length of the beast's torso.

"Not thee," SB intoned.

It flashed again. And again. And a final time, dealing the death blow as the nasty critter squirmed sideways in an attempt to escape.

In a slow-motion but inevitable glide, the worm's lower half slid into the huge crevice and fell silently out of view.

Grym leaped from the beast as it started to fall.

I lowered the sword to my side, panting with exhaustion. Staggering away from the edge of the crevice, I dropped the blade with a clatter.

Grym crouched beside me, his massive chest heaving from his efforts.

"Miss?" Hobs suddenly appeared next to us, Slimy still clutched carefully in his long fingers and a strange expression on his face. He wasn't looking at Grym and me.

Instead, his attention was fixed on the small figure on the other side of the crevice.

Opie stood with his hands clasped before him, his tiny face pleasant under the adorable sprinkling of freckles. He cocked his head at us as SB settled down on my shoulder. "Is that your bird?"

I reached up and touched SB's foot, willing him not to color the air blue in his usual fashion. "A friend. Not a pet," I told the small boy.

Opie nodded, his gaze sliding toward the sword. He frowned. "Did you kill the worm?"

I wasn't wild about the idea of admitting to him that I'd killed something, so I evaded. I could be good at evading if I needed to be. Yes I could.

"He was trying to hurt us."

Opie seemed to think about that for a minute. Then he said. "Pa don't want me to hurt the animals."

I nodded. "That's a good rule of thumb." If Opie had been an adult, he'd have seen the giant gap in my response. Since he wasn't, he seemed much more interested in the bird. "He's pretty."

I glanced at SB and noted the return of his vibrant plumage. "He is, isn't he?"

Beware the child, sayeth Confucius the Frog.

I waved a hand at him to acknowledge that I'd heard. But I was finding it really hard to be afraid of someone with freckles sprinkled across his nose.

Then I remembered Sebille. Okay, addendum... unless they're Sebille.

Opie walked forward, heading right for the deadly crevice. I opened my mouth to tell him to stay back, but the ground healed itself before him, becoming solid just as he settled a tiny, bare foot onto the dirt. "I ain't never had a bird that big. I had a bird once. His name was Dickie. But he wasn't big like this one. Can I have him?"

I shook my head. "He's not mine to give," I said.

The fixtures in the cavern flickered, painting the boy's petulant face with a sickly hue. "But I want him. If'n I want him, I should get him."

Naida, beware the child, Slimy repeated.

I bit back a flare of irritation. Did the frog think I was an idiot?

Scratch that question. Of course he did.

"Now, I think your pa the Sheriff taught you better than that," I said. "But maybe you can help us since you're here. I need to know what makes this place work. Can you show me?" I figured since the kid seemed to spend so much time down there, he'd probably seen something.

He kept glaring at SB as he shook his head, his expression mulish. "I'll trade ya for the bird."

Sighing, I looked at SB. I supposed I could pretend to give him to Opie. He'd come back with me and the sword in the end. I widened my eyes at SB, and he lifted his wings, squawking loudly as he fluttered across the ten feet between the kid and me, landing on Opie's shoulder.

Opie grinned widely, showing slightly crooked teeth, and fed SB a piece of cracker he pulled from his pocket. "Such a pretty bird."

I moved closer, smiling. "Now, can you show me what makes this place run?"

Opie lifted his smile from SB and stared at me. He laughed, a happy sound. "You know, ain't nobody else got this close."

I blinked, unsure what he was telling me. "I'm sorry?"

"Ain't nobody got down here. Ain't nobody kilt the worm. You was the first." He frowned. "I reckon I'll need ta tighten the protections after this."

Alarm spiked through me. I'd hoped I could keep the boy calm until he told me. But apparently the creature who ran the artifact only looked like a child. He clearly didn't have a child's ability to be distracted and bribed.

SB gave another squawk and tried to lift from the boy's shoulder, but Opie grabbed his legs and held him, laughing meanly as he struggled.

"Hobs?" I murmured.

The hobgoblin flashed forward and away, leaving a confused looking Opie with empty hands in his wake. Hobs and the parrot reappeared near the opposite wall.

Opie's expression turned mulish. "You shouldn't oughta done that," he said, his voice turning breathy and deepening on the words.

Something's happening, Slimy warned in my mind.

Grym moved closer. "I think we need to get out of here, Naida keeper."

Before my gaze, the boy's face elongated, widening at the top, and grew exponentially, along with his body. His form spread out thirty feet behind him, rounding as it lengthened. His eyes were slanted silver slits above a square snout. And when the snout opened, massive fangs dripped venom that sizzled on the ground.

And it was only five feet away.

"Run!" Grym screamed, grabbing my wrist and tugging me along with him.

The snake hissed, its tongue snapping out to taste the air inches from my face. I dove for Blackbeard's sword, but the snake was too fast. The reptile punched the blade with its snout, sending it flying away from me. I threw up my hand and called it back, but the snake was there when it hit my palm, its enormous head slamming into me and sending me flying back across the room.

Grym disappeared on a shout of pain and the snake slithered after me so quickly I'd barely slammed into the floor before it was on me again.

I squealed as the terrifying silver gaze appeared above me, the snake's musky odor filling the air I was frantically sucking into my lungs.

Panic turned my muscles to mush and made my heart pound painfully in my chest. I went very still as the snake's snout opened and the testing tongue slipped toward me, stopping just above my face and throbbing there.

Itsssssss time for you to die, keeper. You've interfered long enough in my plansssssss.

The sibilant tone skimmed silkily across my nerves, making gooseflesh rise along my skin. I was a heartbeat away from death. I knew it with every pound of my heart...with every thought skittering wildly through my mind.

I would die.

My friends would die.

And the magical creatures who'd been trapped within the poisonous artifact would either die or continue on as prisoners.

The purse! a voice said in my brain. It took me a moment to connect the voice to Slimy. Then I realized what he'd said.

"What plans did I interfere with?" I asked the snake as I slowly slid my hand into my waistband and removed the purse, dropping it alongside my body where the snake wouldn't see it. The problem with being very close to something is that it's harder to see the thing you're close to.

The snake's tongue slipped out again, as if testing the genuineness of my question. *The world isssssssss mine. I must always grow it, leech it of color, make it my own, personal heaven. You tried to sssssssstop me. That'sssssssss not nicccccccce.*

The snout dipped closer, the nasty forked tongue slipped over my face and I grimaced, my fingers desperately digging inside the purse. In desperation,

I jerked the first item my fingers touched out of the purse.

The snake reared back, head tilting in question as I yanked the tissue forward and flapped it on the air.

Oops!

Without missing a beat, I ran the tissue across my face, wiping off the snake spit. "Um, I don't like to be wet."

The silver eyes narrowed, the huge body tensed.

"Naida," Grym shouted from somewhere out of view. "Quit screwing around!"

I huffed. *Gobbling Gargoyle goobers*! I'd like to see him deal with about a thousand pounds of snake perched in his lap.

The snake suddenly reared up with an enraged roar. Snake spittle sprayed the area as the monster whipped its head around.

Grym was dancing alongside the huge reptile with Blackbeard's sword in his hand, slashing and slicing along the thick scaly form.

I used the distraction to scramble backward and away. I needed the flashlight. I needed to get to that purse!

Unfortunately, there was a thousand pounds of reptile dancing around on top of it as the snake fought the gargoyle.

"Sizzling snake spit, Grym! There's not going to be anything left of the bag after you get done!"

He slashed at the snake and danced away, a glare on his rocky face. "I'm doing the best I can, Naida."

The snake struck, faster than words, and Grym was suddenly clutched between its jaws.

He yelled as the nasty thing lifted its enormous head, clearly intending to swallow him whole.

"Grym!"

The flash! A tiny voice in my head said. And I scurried out of my hidey-hole to find it. The snake had moved a little, and I could just see the edge of the sparkly silver purse in the dust. I reached for it and the snake rolled backward as Grym slashed at its face with the sword.

I retreated quickly to avoid being crushed beneath the massive body.

SB joined the fray, slashing at the snake's silver eyes with his talons.

The snake flung its head up on a hissing roar and Grym went flying, knocking SB out of the air on the way.

I didn't watch to see if they landed okay, the snake lifted off the bag and I dove in and grabbed it, scrabbling for the latch.

I caught movement out of the corner of my eye, but I didn't have enough time to get out of the way. The enormous head slammed into me, shoving me into a glowing rock formation so hard it knocked all the air out of my lungs.

The snake slithered closer, blood painting its

charcoal gray head in glossy strips. *That'sssss it! I'm done being patient, Keeper. Now you die!*

I couldn't breathe. I made screeching noises as I tried to draw air into my screaming chest. My eyesight dimmed and my legs gave out from the lack of air. All I wanted to do was roll up into the fetal position and fight to breathe. But I couldn't do it.

I had one more job to do.

My fingers digging frantically inside the purse, I prayed the flash hadn't been shattered into tiny little pieces.

The snake slammed into me again, pressing me into the rock with its snout, a triumphant gleam in the slanted gaze.

Agony speared through me. Bones cracked under the impact. Stars burst and my vision turned charcoal gray around the edges.

My fingers touched the flashlight.

I released my grip on the purse, opening my mouth to wheeze against the pressure in my chest. And, lifting my terrified gaze to the snake's triumphant one, I clicked the flashlight on.

Sssssssso long, Keeper, the snake hissed out.

I sucked a noisy breath and said. "Later!"

I slid my finger over the lever on the side and pointed it at the snake.

The reptile reared up and back, eyes widening in fear. Fangs snapped the air as it tried to close its maw over the small, metal canister. But the pink illumination somehow held it back. The enormous reptile shimmered violently inside the perfect arc of pale-rose light.

I coughed forcefully, fighting to hold the light on the beast as it lifted off the ground, spiraling into the air, and faded away on the heels of an enraged hiss.

Silence filled the cavern for a long moment, then someone groaned, long and low.

I shoved to my knees, finally managing to pull air into my lungs. Another groan drew my gaze to Grym.

My eyes widened and, unbelievably, I laughed. Dragging myself to my feet, I stumbled toward the gargoyle, my chest screaming. "I'd give anything for Sebille's phone right now so I could get a picture."

Grym blinked and looked down at himself.

He was clutching the parrot in his arms like a newborn babe.

With a sough of air, the sword lying on the ground beside him rose into the air and found me, smacking into my uplifted hand with a familiar heft.

Hobs was suddenly beside me. "Miss, you did it!"

I looked where the snake had been, all too cognizant of the last time I'd banished it with the light. "It probably won't last," I told him. "We need to get everybody down here, fast." I squeezed his shoulder. "Do you think you can do that?"

He nodded and was gone in a blur of motion.

I sank to the ground, leaning heavily against the rock and holding my agony-filled middle.

"You all right?" Grym asked, not looking any better than I felt.

"I will be as soon as we get out of this goddess-forsaken place."

Grym nodded and closed his eyes. "I couldn't agree more."

I closed my eyes too. I'd just rest for a few minutes. Just a few min...

23

WHERE'S MY PURSE?

I awoke to the sound of giggling. Somebody was poking me on the shoulder.

Poke. Giggle. Poke. Giggle.

A heavy warmth pressed against my stomach and something rumbled through my insides.

I swiped at the poking finger and grumbled. "Leave me alone."

Poke, poke, poke, giggle.

"Argh!" Slapping the hand away, I jolted upright, my eyes snapping open. Then my mouth.

"Meow!" Wicked walked up my chest and rubbed his soft head against my chin, purring loudly enough to vibrate my lungs.

The cavern was filled with people. It looked as if Hobs had managed to get everyone from the artifact into the cavern.

There were people dressed as cowboys and Indians. People dressed as aliens from outer space. And people dressed as country folks from 1960s television. "Holy goddess's last pair of clean undies," I muttered.

I looked up into the hobgoblin's smiling face. "How did you...?"

He shrugged. "We all worked together, Miss."

I recognized a few of the people from Lea's neighborhood who'd been like zombies before. They seemed aware and slightly confused and excited all at once.

I glanced at Lea. My friend smiled. "As soon as they came in here, they remembered their real lives." She shook her head, looking sad. "Some of them have been here a lifetime. Everything they once knew could be gone when they get home."

I reached up and clasped her hand, giving it a squeeze. "We don't know how time works in this thing," I told her. "Maybe it will be like they were only gone a few minutes."

Then another thought occurred. I looked at Sebille and Rustin. "Will they all go back where they were taken from?" I asked.

Rustin shrugged. "There was nothing about returning people in the texts I read. Nobody's ever come back from one of these things before."

I sighed. "Well, I guess we'll find out. If they all end up at Croakies, we'll just have to help them find their way home."

Sebille frowned but nodded.

Grym offered me his hand. I noticed he'd returned to his human form and somebody had given him a pair of ill-fitting slacks. The good news was that they didn't fit any worse than the pants he'd arrived in. They were too tight across his muscular thighs and three inches too short. He'd shoved Blackbeard's sword into the belt and had SB perched on his shoulder, resembling a handsome, well-groomed pirate.

I squinted at Grym's slacks. "Are those from a Sheriff's uniform?"

Grym flushed. "Yeah. Sheriff Andrew was kind enough to share them."

I felt my eyes go wide. "You told Sheriff Andrew? Do you think that was a good idea?"

"Bwawk!" SB squawked. "Never invite yer enemies ta taste yer rum, or ye'll find yourself without grog and thrown to yer bum."

"Exactly," I agreed. "I think."

Barney Fiff waved at me from the center of the crowd. Standing next to him, Polly winked at Grym and glared at me.

"Keeper!" A familiar voice called. I turned as a man and a women walked out of the crowd. My pulse spiked as I saw it was the Sheriff and Aunt Bee.

Both were smiling widely. Aunt Bee bustled up to me and held out a plate with a slice of pie on it. "Here. I've been sharing it around."

I lifted my hands and took a step back. "Um. No. Thank you. I'm not risking it."

She laughed good-naturedly. "It's safe as can be." She pointed to the plate, which I noticed had a fine crack down the center which had been repaired. "This isn't from the artifact." She beamed up at the Sheriff. "Dear Andy found it and glued it together for me. I believe it might belong to you...Keeper."

The Sheriff nodded. "We owe you a giant debt, Keeper. If you and your friends hadn't come along..." He shook his head, sighing. "Well, we might have been here a very long time. Maybe forever."

I took his offered hand. "We didn't do it alone," I told him. "There were people here who helped."

He nodded. "I'm really glad they managed to evade me." He looked ashamed.

Grym patted him on the back. "Not your fault. You didn't know about the no eating thing. It was a fluke that they figured it out before they were poisoned too."

"Well, thank goodness they did," Aunt Bee said. She frowned. "About Opie..."

I shook my head. "He was never real. He was just a figment. A hologram. "

She shook her head, sighing. "I always knew there was something wrong with that boy."

I patted her arm. "Yeah, he definitely seemed a bit off." I didn't tell her I'd begun to suspect the boy when he'd showed up at the diner and talked about electricity. Then, when I'd gotten that radio message in the hut, the realization had hit me how right the young boy was. Electricity ran the world. It was invisible. Deadly. Saturating the very air around us. Energy was electrical. Magical too. It was at the heart of everything.

He'd been taunting us with the message. Far too clever for a small child. But not for an arrogant entity.

I looked at my friends. "We need to get out of here," I told them "That snake can fight its way back."

"Any ideas how to do that?" Rustin asked.

I nodded. "Where's my purse?"

Sebille lifted her eyebrows. "Your purse? Since when do you carry a purse?"

Grym handed me the sparkly clutch. "Since *this* answered my call," I told her.

The sprite ogled the purse. "Is that another one of those endless stuff bags?" Sebille and I had come across an endless stuff artifact when we'd gone to the Plex dimension to save Hobs and Slimy. Long story... Suffice it to say it was a handy type of artifact to have around. But it required a little creativity to use.

"Better. This is a variation on the burlap sack. Apparently, it carries only the things you're going to need for any given task. I just had to figure out how to use them."

I reached inside and pulled out the key, holding it up. "This is the only thing in here I haven't used."

My friends all looked around for a door.

I shook my head. "It's over here." I worked my way through the crowd of the artifact's victims, not difficult because they pretty much split apart and let us through.

I headed for the strip of rocky wall where my keeper magics disappeared when I sent them looking for SB and the sword. My rationale was that the entire goal and purpose of the artifact was to create and maintain artificial worlds. The biggest part of that was hiding reality.

Every "presentation" the artifact provided was a facade, with reality sitting behind it. Like the Behind the Scenes area where Dugan and the rebels had held out while trying to beat the artifact.

As if my thought had pulled him forward, Dugan stepped out of the crowd and, with a wide smile and a nod of his head, he fell in beside me as I headed for the wall.

I stopped in front of the spot where I thought the door would be and held out the key.

Nothing happened for a beat. And then another. I was starting to second-guess myself when I noticed that the "rock" at the center of the space looked smeared, its color slowly changing from gray stone to warm wood. A moment later, we were all looking at a door.

A cheer rose up behind me. Dugan clapped me on the shoulder. Grym, Sebille, Rustin, and Lea moved up behind me for moral support.

Taking a deep breath, I inserted the key into the lock on the door.

Silence throbbed as I reached for the knob, clasped it, and started to turn.

A blood-curdling scream sounded at the back of the cavern.

I jerked around to see the snake rising from the dust near the passage entrance, its slanted silver gaze narrowing on me. Without warning, the monster shot forward, spearing through the crowd directly at me.

"Naida!" Grym screamed.

People leaped out of the striking snake's way, a few of them slammed into the floor by the violence of its passing. Screams reverberated through the underground space, echoing off the walls and slashing back to slice painfully at my eardrums.

I stared into the snake's irate gaze, an odd calm sliding over me.

And opened the door.

I smiled.

With a final glance over my shoulder, I reached inside.

The snake's enormous form left the ground, its coils snapping straight to give it distance, and its venomous maw opened wide.

I wrapped my fingers around the fist-sized plug in the wall before me and tugged.

The green lights of the cavern flickered and died.

The snake struck, fangs dripping, and the musky scent of reptile filled my senses as the enormous snake enclosed me in its maw.

And then flashed into nothing on a burst of eerie green light.

I blinked, halfway shocked I was still alive.

The silence broke on a wild cheer as everyone realized the danger was over.

And even better. We were all going home.

As the last victim stepped through the door, disappearing into the gray mist that would take them to their own homes, I glanced over at my friends. Most of them had stayed with me, waiting until everyone else was safely away before we left the artifact.

Because of what Sindra and Dolfo had told us, I had a strong suspicion that once I left the artifact it would be destroyed. And I didn't want to risk leaving anybody behind if that happened.

So, I'd waited to the end to leave.

Dugan had left once and stuck his head back through to give us the happy news that Enchanted waited on the other end of the gray mist. Then he'd promptly disappeared, after declaring he was off digital entertainment forever. From that point on, he told us, he was only going to deal with things he could hold in his hands. Like books.

I wisely refrained from telling him about the book artifacts I had at Croakies that could suck a person into the world of the book and keep them there.

I'd leave him with his false sense of security. At least until or if he started collecting old and rare books. Then I might need to warn him.

"Okay, you guys," I told my friends. "Your turn."

"Thank the goddess," Sebille said, tugging on her weird skirt, which I was amused to see she'd never changed out of. "I can't wait to get into my real clothes. No more being the fashionable laughing stock in the neighborhood."

Lea and I shared a wide grin at that statement, but all I said was, "Yep, tall striped socks are virtual wallflower garb."

Sebille eyed me as if trying to decide if I was making fun of her and then seemed to decide it didn't matter. She slipped past me and disappeared into the mist. Rustin and Lea, who was carrying Hex, were right behind her. Hobs rushed through with a war-whoop, Slimy bug-eyed and croaking in his long-fingered grip.

A warm softness wound around my ankles. I looked down at Mr. Wicked and smiled. Scooping him up, I hugged him close, kissing him between the ears. "Ready to go home, buddy?"

"Yes," said a gruff voice beside me. I looked up in surprise, finding Grym grinning at me, wearing only his bare chest and too-tight pants.

It was a good look for him. A very good look. And I had to clamp my lips together to keep from telling him so.

"Your turn," I told the gargoyle.

He shook his head. "We're going through together. If anything else jumps up to try to stop you at the last minute..."

"We haven't been attacked by a giant rabid butterfly yet," I told him, frowning thoughtfully.

Grinning, Grym looped his arm through mine. "I wouldn't even be surprised. Hanging around with you is always an adventure Naida."

My grin faded. "Is that a bad thing?"

Grym didn't respond. His eyes twinkling mischievously, he tugged me into the mist, wrapping himself around me.

Before we stepped out into Croakies, I felt the soft, warm press of his lips against mine. The kiss was brief, so brief I thought for a moment that I'd imagined it. But it had been nice.

Really nice.

Magical even.

The End

READ MORE ENCHANTING INQUIRIES

If you enjoyed **Black & White Croakies**, you might want to check out the rest of the series. Please enjoy Chapter One of **Unbaked Croakies**, the PREQUEL for the *Enchanting Inquiries* as my gift to you!

How in the name of the goddess's favorite sports bra am I going to do this Magical Librarian job?

I have no idea what I'm doing. And the woman who's supposed to be training me is...well, let's just say she's distracted and leave it at that. I guess I'll bumble through. It's become something of a trademark move for me. *Holy Bat boogers*! I could really use a cat and a frog. Too bad I don't have either!

UNBAKED CROAKIES - PREQUEL

CHAPTER ONE
Oy, Pudsy. How's things?

I stood on the street outside the bookstore, frowning up at the ugly wood sign with the picture of a spotted frog on it. The yellowed white paint was chipped and scarred, and there was a black blotch near the frog's mouth that looked like a fly.

I kept expecting the frog's tongue to snake out and snap it up.

It was an ugly sign. World-class ugly. But it was oddly suited given the store's strange name.

Croakies.

I mean. What kind of name was that for a bookstore?

Soft footsteps came up behind me and I resisted turning.

"Are you ready?"

At just under six feet, the man was only a few inches taller than I was. I guessed he was about middle age. For a sorcerer that would put him in his eighties or nineties. He had piercing blue eyes that were a little darker than mine and longish, curly brown hair. He also had a truly forgettable face. I mean that literally. From one moment to the next I would often forget what the man looked like. In fact, the few times I'd seen him, I'd only been able to identify him because of the sorcerer's garb he wore.

The thought made me frown.

I always remembered the piercing blue gaze. And the hair. But that was all that stuck in my mind.

I knew him only as Agent A.P. from the Société of Dire Magic. A formidable group whose moniker seemed to strike fear into the hearts of everyone I spoke to about them. Supernormals, at least. Since I'd been raised by a non-magical grandmother, I didn't really know that many supernormals. But the few I'd met since A.P. had knocked on my door a couple of weeks earlier, had seemed more than half afraid of him.

I had no idea what it was that scared them about the man. He seemed harmless enough to me.

I turned to look at the agent. He was less intimidating in his street clothes than he'd been in his robes. I'd only met him a handful of times. But each time we'd met previous to when he'd come to fetch me from my grandmother's home a little while ago, he'd looked just like a fairytale sorcerer in his long purple and black robes. All that had been missing was the pointy hat.

And the wand.

When I'd jokingly asked him where those two items were, he'd very earnestly explained that they were only for special ceremonies.

I hadn't known him long enough to recognize if he was joking.

I chose to believe he was.

Otherwise, it would just be too weird.

But back to his question. *Was I ready?*

Taking a deep, bracing breath, I nodded. I was as ready as I was ever going to be. With a feeling that my life was about to change in ways I couldn't imagine and might not like, I reached for the door to Croakies and opened it.

A mangy black cat galloped toward the door as it opened, yowling as if he were being chased by an army of slavering canines. The feline's headlong flight was accompanied by a prolonged shriek.

"Banshee Botox!" a woman caterwauled from deep inside the store. "Close the door! Don't let him out."

I quickly slammed the door behind me, cutting the agent behind me off in mid-stride.

A.P. yelped in pain from the wrong side of the entrance.

A woman came scurrying out of the stacks, rushing over to grab the cat, who was almost as big as a full-sized dachshund and sported only one and a half ears.

The feline's longish black fur was matted and sparse in spots, making him look like he'd spent the better part his life on the streets. White fur speckled the big cat's cheeks and chin, marking him as a feline of the older variety. His large, expressive eyes were a silvery-green and probably the prettiest thing about him.

Which wasn't saying much.

"Fenwald, you naughty boy," the woman said, her accent strident and British.

She looked at me through a pair of large tortoise-shell glasses, shoving them up a pug nose and peering at me as if I were a particularly nasty bug. "What is it, then? Do ya need a book?"

The door behind me opened, and A.P. came inside the store, rubbing his decidedly red nose. He glared at the woman behind the square glasses. "Alice. That cat is a menace."

I expected her to buckle under his severe disappointment. Instead, she grinned.

"Oy, Pudsy. How's things? You're looking a bit pinkish about the old snout there, eh?" Her laughter was a series of odd snorts that vibrated the glasses down her nose. She reached up and poked them back into place with a bandaged finger covered in black ink. "Ah," she said, her smallish brown eyes rolling back to me. "So, this is my new apprentice, then?" She looked me over with a critical eye. "She'll do." The woman offered me a work-roughened hand. "I'm Alice, Keeper of the Artifacts. You're Naida?"

I nodded, struck dumb by the reality in front of me. In my mind, I'd pictured a tall, powerful woman with a calm, no-nonsense manner as Keeper. Alice wasn't any of those things.

Jerking her head toward the side, Alice said. "Come on, then. I'll make us a spot of tea." She carried the big cat with her as she slouched toward a nook across from the sales counter. The space sported a miniature stove and a short counter, which was covered in tea-making things. The oven door was open, and a comfortable warmth oozed from its interior. The cat immediately sprawled in front of it and began to bathe, clearly enjoying the heat.

With a jolt, I realized Alice was using the ancient appliance to warm the bookstore. "Is the heater broken?" I asked, pulling my coat closer as I shivered. I wasn't looking forward to spending a winter shivering and sniffling day and night.

Alice flipped a dismissive hand. "It's just having a fit. It'll be right as rain in no time."

I sent A.P. a worried glance, and he shook his head. "You need to get that fixed, Alice," he told the woman. "It was part of your apprenticeship agreement with the Société."

She ignored him completely, motioning negligently toward the small, three-person table in the center of the open space at the front of the store. A high, narrow window above the tea nook showed the clear blue of an early-January sky. The bright sunshine painted a golden ribbon across the bookstore's ratty carpet and bathed the round table in warmth. "Have a seat, sweetums." She glanced at A.P. "You too, Pudsy. I'll have tea ready in two shakes."

I looked at A.P. and smiled, mouthing, "Pudsy?"

He shook his head dismissively.

While the tea steeped, Alice pulled the oven door wide. Grabbing a dingy towel that was appliqued with a large black cat that looked nothing like Fenwald, she tugged a flat pan from the oven's interior. She carefully extracted three pale, oblong biscuits from the pan, arranging them like spokes on a wheel in the center of a chipped white plate and sliding the rest back inside the oven.

Alice placed the snack on the table between us. "Scones. My specialty."

Having missed breakfast that morning, I smiled in anticipation. "Thank you. They smell delicious."

Alice gave me a pleased smile and returned to her tea prep.

Fenwald wandered over and sat down a few feet

away from the table, staring at me through an unfathomable green gaze.

I reached for a scone, eyeing the dark spots marking its golden surface and wondering what they were. I hoped they weren't raisins. *Maybe blueberries?* I thought, hopefully.

A.P. reached out and touched my hand with a finger, shaking his head and frowning as I lifted it toward my mouth.

Grinning, I took a bite.

"Ow!" I said before I could stop myself.

A.P. sat back and shook his head.

"Watch out, sweetums. They're hot."

I pulled the scone from my mouth and looked at the shallow dent my teeth had made in it. Feeling my front teeth to make sure they were still intact, I arched my brows at A.P.

He chuckled soundlessly. Reaching for another scone, he held it above the table for a moment, glancing over at Alice, he asked, "Is that a new thriller section, Alice?"

The Keeper lifted her head and looked into the bookstore. "Yes. Blimey, you do have a keen eye. I moved them from the back because I've seen new interest in thrillers of late." Alice wandered over to the books in question and ran her hand lovingly over their perfectly arranged spines.

While she was distracted. The Société agent slammed his scone against the edge of the table, coughing loudly to cover the noise, and broke a large chunk off the end of it. He threw the piece to Fenwald. It hit the carpet with the weight of a large marble and skittered to a spot a few inches from the cat.

Fenwald eyed the heavy offering and then lifted a derisive gaze to A.P., as if to say, *I'm not eating that.* Not wasting any time considering the offering, the big cat reached out with a large paw and whacked it away.

We watched it skitter beneath the cabinet where Alice kept her assortment of teas, out of sight.

I wondered how many other bits of bad baking the cat had "stored" beneath the cabinet. Then I decided I probably didn't want to know.

"I find I'm growing fond of the genre," Alice said, oblivious as she returned to her tea-making. She glanced over her shoulder at me. "How about you, Naida? What's your favorite genre?"

I flushed in embarrassment, not wanting to tell her in front of A.P. "Um, paranormal." It wasn't a lie...exactly...I did like some paranormal along with my romance.

Alice's grin widened. "A fine choice. I have a large selection in the store. Help yourself if you'd like. Just be sure to put a couple of dollars in the till for the rent."

My eyes went wide. "Rent?" There'd been no mention of rent. I'd thought I was going to be working off my room and board. It was an old-fashioned arrangement but a necessity. When my grandmother had died a few months previous, she'd left me with a tiny house filled with ratty furnishings and a lot of debt that pretty much wiped out whatever I would earn from the sale of the house.

I had no money and no family that I knew of. If Agent A.P. hadn't come to me and told me there was an apprenticeship open for an artifact librarian, I'd have been in sad shape.

For once in my life, it had seemed like the winds of fate had blown in my favor. Though the Societe agent had been vague about how he'd found me, murmuring something about being a friend of my grandmother's.

I highly doubted that.

"Yes," said Alice. "I rent books for avid readers who don't have the space to store them all."

I nodded in understanding. "That makes sense."

She placed cups of tea in front of us and then pulled a third chair from the corner. Dropping into it with a sigh, Alice Parker fixed a speculative look on me. Then, lifting her teacup to her mouth, she said, "So, Naida Griffith, tell me why I should hire you as an apprentice for Keeper of the Artifacts?"

My mind went blank. I glanced toward A.P., but he wasn't paying attention to us. He'd pulled out his cell phone and seemed to be checking his emails.

I was on my own.

"Um..." I said stupidly. I tucked a long strand of my curly brown hair behind one ear. Digging deep, I discarded options as quickly as they occurred to me. I couldn't tell her it was because I'd just turned twenty-two and needed a job. From what A.P. had told me, Keepers were born to wrangle artifacts. It wasn't a career choice. It was their legacy. I didn't want Alice to know I wasn't really suited for the job. She'd find out soon enough.

After a moment that stretched farther than the last pair of size eight jeans I'd tried to pull on over my size ten hips, I finally said the only thing that came to mind. "Strange objects seem to follow me around." I cringed inwardly. As random statements went, it was somewhere in the realm of "I see dead people."

To my shock, Alice cocked her head, narrowed her small eyes behind the massive glasses, and smiled. "Well now, that's just perfect. Okay then. Let's get started."

Check out the entire series here: https://samcheever. com/books/#enchanting

ALSO BY SAM CHEEVER

If you enjoyed **Black & White Croakies**, you might also enjoy these other fun mystery series by Sam. To find out more, visit the **BOOKS** page at www.samcheever.com:

Enchanting Inquiries Paranormal Mysteries - **For more fun adventures with Naida, Sebille, Wicked, Slimy, and Hobs!**
Reluctant Familiar Paranormal Mysteries
Yesterday's Paranormal Mysteries
Gainfully Employed Mysteries
Silver Hills Cozy Mysteries
Country Cousin Mysteries

ABOUT THE AUTHOR

USA Today and WSJ Bestselling Author Sam Cheever writes contemporary and paranormal mystery and suspense, creating stories that draw you in and keep you eagerly turning pages. Known for writing great characters, snappy dialogue, and unique and exhilarating stories, Sam is the award-winning author of 80+ books.

To learn more about Sam and her work, visit her at one of her online hotspots:
www.samcheever.com
samcheever@samcheever.com